MAR - - 2022

iZZY NEWTON AND THE S.M.A.R.T. SQUAD

NEWTON'S FLAW

VALERIE TRIPP

Illustrated by Geneva Bowers

UNDER THE Stars

NATIONAL GEOGRAPHIC

NATIONAL GEOGRAPHIC and Yellow Border Design are trademarks of the National Geographic Society, used under license.

Under the Stars is a trademark of National Geographic Partners, LLC.

Since 1888, the National Geographic Society has funded more than 14,000 research, conservation, education, and storytelling projects around the world. National Geographic Partners distributes a portion of the funds it receives from your purchase to National Geographic Society to support programs including the conservation of animals and their habitats. To learn more, visit natgeo.com/info.

For more information, visit nationalgeographic.com, call 1-877-873-6846, or write to the following address:

National Geographic Partners, LLC
1145 17th Street N.W.
Washington, DC 20036-4688 U.S.A.

For librarians and teachers: nationalgeographic.com/books/librarians-and-educators/

More for kids from National Geographic: natgeokids.com

National Geographic Kids magazine inspires children to explore their world with fun yet educational articles on animals, science, nature, and more. Using fresh storytelling and amazing photography, *Nat Geo Kids* shows kids ages 6 to 14 the fascinating truth about the world—and why they should care. **kids.nationalgeographic.com/subscribe**

For rights or permissions inquiries, please contact National Geographic Books Subsidiary Rights: bookrights@natgeo.com

Designed by Julide Dengel
Illustrations by Geneva Bowers

Hardcover ISBN: 978-1-4263-7153-0
Reinforced library binding ISBN: 978-1-4263- 7154-7

Printed in the United States of America
21/WOR/1

For my friend Don Vannoy and
my grandniece Helen Heuer,
with tremendous thanks for their help.
—Valerie Tripp

It's never impossible
to follow your dreams!
—Geneva Bowers

Izzy Newton had a secret, and it was cosmic. Only two other people in the entire universe knew about it—her brothers. They'd known all summer, and they were totally trustworthy, so Izzy was sure that her secret was safe until the day she decided to spring it on the world, which ... Izzy grinned. Might be *today*.

Izzy's friend Marie Curie saw her beaming smile and asked, "What?"

"Oh, nothing," said Izzy, even though she was bursting to tell. A breeze tousled her curls and twisted the strings of her hoodie. She and her friends were on the flat roof of their school building. They had discovered how to get there back in September when they first started sixth grade at Atom Middle School.

Now it was October. It was the first sunny day in a week, and the girls had rushed up after lunch to enjoy a few minutes of sunshine before their afternoon classes. Izzy felt on top of the world—or at least the part of it that mattered to *her*. She sighed, "Isn't this place The Best?"

"It's great," said Marie.

" 'Great' doesn't touch it," corrected Allie Einstein. "The roof is great multiplied by googolplex. You can see the whole wide world from up here."

Charlie Darwin didn't say anything. She was doing a series of warm-up exercises, raising her arms high over her head, taking deep breaths of the warm October air.

The girls had transformed a protected corner into a private hangout. Pooling their talents, they'd created a habitat that was part jungle, part greenscape. Charlie, who was really into biology, had transplanted pumpkin vines into long wooden boxes. Marie, crazy for chemistry, had used compost to concoct an organic fertilizer so potent the pumpkin vines went bonkers, overflowing the boxes. Physicist Izzy had made pinwheels that stopped the birds from pecking at the tiny pumpkins. And Allie, the math whiz, had written a computer program to measure hours of sunlight and their effect on the pumpkins' growth.

Just then, their friend Gina Carver burst through the door. She was wearing her backpack, which—like her locker, pockets, room at home, and brain—was overstuffed and overflowing with a crazy collection of things and ideas for her potential engineering projects. Gina knelt beside the contraption she'd invented to collect rainwater and automatically sprinkle it on the pumpkin plants on dry days. "How's it working?" she asked.

"It's dripping beautifully," said Izzy.

Suddenly, a piece of paper flew out of Gina's backpack. Allie caught it just as it swirled up into the sky. As she read the paper, Allie shouted, "Guess what, guess what, guess *what*!? There's going to be a pop-up science fair!"

ATOM MIDDLE SCHOOL'S
Pop-up SCIENCE
FAIR

The Countdown Has Begun:
Atom Middle School's Pop-up Science Fair blasts off in ten days!
Be ready to launch your project.
Ignite your imaginations!
Get your brains fired up!

"The Countdown Has Begun: Atom Middle School's Pop-up Science Fair blasts off in ten days! Be ready to launch your project. Ignite your imaginations! Get your brains fired up!" Allie read from the paper.

"Say again?" said Charlie, upside down in a headstand.

"What's that?" asked Marie.

"A pop-up science fair," Allie repeated impatiently, waving the paper above her head. Her bright blond hair stood up as if electrified, looking as excited as Allie sounded. "It's only the coolest thing ever."

"Never heard of it," said Marie.

"Where have you been living, Marie?" asked Allie. "Under a rock?"

"No," said Marie tartly. "I lived in Paris the last two years, remember?"

"As if you would ever let us forget it," said Allie, rolling her eyes.

Izzy leapt in to keep the peace. "My brothers told me about pop-ups. They're sort of like a combination race and contest and exhibition."

"I don't get it," said Charlie.

Allie explained, "Instead of the same old, same old science fair experiments that drag on forever, the idea is that you get only 10 days from start to finish to do your project. Bing, bang, bong."

"More like the way it is for working scientists," said Izzy, "who have to produce under time pressure. Or think of the astronauts on Apollo 13, where they had a do-or-die deadline to fix the module or be lost in space."

"When does the countdown to this pop-up thing start?" asked ever-practical Gina.

"Now!" cheered Allie, raising both arms.

"*¡Fabuloso!*" said Charlie, still upside down.

"Get a load of us, excited about a time-sensitive science fair," laughed Marie. "Are we geeks or what?" She pointed to the rooftop pumpkin patch. "Any normal person would say that up here, the science fair has already begun. You've got a head start, Gina. You can enter your rain catcher."

"No, no, no," Allie contradicted. "We should do a project *together*. The five of us, one project, right?"

"Savage," said Gina. The other girls were used to Gina's hipster way of flipping words so that they meant the opposite of what they usually meant. In this case, "savage" meant "fantastic." "We'll *dominate*," said Gina.

"We," said Charlie with calm confidence, "will blow everybody else out of the water." She lowered her feet to the ground with sinewy grace. Her thick brown braid and bangs settled into place as she stood upright and stretched to her full height, which was tall. "I think Marie is onto something. We should take advantage of what we've begun on the roof. Our project should be something important. It should be about protecting the environment, like measuring the effect of roof grass on lowering heating and cooling bills."

"Or the benefits of a rainscape," said Gina, pushing her glasses up the bridge of her nose.

"Or using wind turbines to power Atom Middle School," suggested Izzy.

"Or the best organic compound for fertilizer," said Marie. "Look how well my rescue plants are doing."

"They're the Plants That Ate Atom Middle School," Izzy joked. "I'd say you have a green thumb, Marie, but really, *all* your fingers are green."

"What can I say?" Marie shrugged, making the sequins on her tee shirt catch the sun and glitter. "It's true." In addition to the pumpkins, Marie also fertilized plants that Allie referred to as "Marie's Sticks." They'd been nearly dead, almost-goners that had been thrown away. Marie had brought them to the roof, repotted them, watered them, fed them compost fertilizer, and brought them—well, some of them—back to life. Izzy thought it was surprising: Marie disliked messes, but she loved getting down and dirty with stinky compost for her rescue plants.

"I don't know why you bother with those pitiful twigs, Marie," said Allie. "Anyway, *puh-lease*. Our science fair project has *got* to be more exciting and glamorous than *fertilizer*."

Allie held the paper up again and pointed to it, saying, "Also, remember, we don't have time for any long-term experiments. We should do something that will take only a few days. Like, how about one day we make a high-speed, stop-action film of the arrival and departure times of the buses, as observed from the roof? And then we could do a computer analysis, and then make a plan for un-jamming all that bus traffic."

"I love the idea of a high-speed film," said Gina. "The buses would look like yellow streaks from here."

"Or maybe lightning bugs," added Charlie, who was a big insect fan. "Because we're up so high."

"Aren't you crazy about this weird old school building?" said Marie. "There's no way we'd be able to have a secret hangout on top of one of the new, streamlined buildings. I just wish we could spend more time up here. A nanosecond after lunch isn't enough."

"Wait until our report cards come out," said Allie. "When we all make Principal's Honor Roll—which, of course, we *will*—we can eat lunch wherever we want. It's one of the privileges you get for getting all A's."

"We'll be able to eat up here," said Gina, "every day."

"Every *nice* day," Marie said, tucking a strand of hair—dyed lime green—behind her ear. "When the sky's clear."

"Yes," said Charlie. She inhaled, stretched her arms out to the sides and then overhead, palms together, in another yoga pose.

Izzy smiled, although there was one teeny, tiny gray cloud in her sky that made her worry about being on the honor roll. She was stuck in a class called Forensics. Izzy shuddered, thinking of what a terrible discovery it had been to find out that the word "forensics" has two very different meanings. She thought it meant the scientific analysis of physical evidence from a crime scene, like in TV shows and movies. *That* would have been one of her all-time favorite classes. Unfortunately, as she had learned to her horror, forensics also means the study of debating and making speeches. More than anything else in the universe, Izzy hated standing up and talking in front of people. The thought of it made her brain cramp. Once, a few weeks ago, she had stood up in front of the cafeteria packed with students and made a pitch for a school STEM team. Somehow she had managed, though the memory of it was a nightmare. But so far, every time she was supposed to speak in Forensics class, she had choked. *Oh, well,* she told herself. Even if she flunked Forensics, her other grades should pull her average up.

Very casually, Izzy asked, "Uh, like, your grades put you on the honor roll, right?"

"Yes, your grades and your effort marks, too" said Allie. "You know: Outstanding, Satisfactory, or Unsatisfactory."

Uh-oh. Izzy couldn't deny that her efforts in Forensics had been Unsatisfactory to the Max. Man, did she ever hate that class. Now it looked like Forensics was not only torture that was slowly killing her, it might ruin her chances for the honor roll, too. Not to mention lunch with her friends on the roof.

"Atom's turned out to be better than Satisfactory, hasn't it?" said Gina, not even looking up from tinkering with her rain catcher.

"I'll say," Allie agreed, "I like all my classes and clubs. I like Pep Squad, too." She cupped her hands around her mouth and whispered, "And I love the S.M.A.R.T. Squad."

"Fist bump," said Izzy. The five girls bumped fists—

Allie adding a dance step as she did—and grinned at one another. In September, they had put their wicked-smart scientific brains to work and solved a mystery about why the school was so cold. They had such a blast that they decided to start a secret mystery-solving team. They called themselves the S.M.A.R.T. Squad, which stood for **S**olving **M**ysteries **A**nd **R**evealing **T**ruths.

"Let's meet after school to start planning our science fair project," said Allie.

"We've got track team," said Gina and Charlie together, pointing to each other.

"I've got to babysit my nephew Crosby," said Marie.

"Bummer," said Allie with exaggerated sympathy.

"Oh, no," Marie protested. "I—"

But Allie ignored Marie and spoke over her, "How about you, Iz?" she asked.

"Wellllll," said Izzy, smiling, but with her eyebrows knotted anxiously, "today's … ice hockey tryouts."

"Oh, right, of course!" said Gina. "I knew you were going to try out, but I forgot tryouts are *today*." She chanted, "Ice hock-ee! Ice hock-ee!"

"You've got this, Izzy," said Charlie. "Nailed."

"I sure do hope so," Izzy replied nervously.

"I *know* so," said Allie, whapping Izzy on the back. "I've told you a gazillion times: You own the ice."

The girls—except for Marie—agreed to meet at the library after their after-school activities to plan for the science fair. As they split up to go to their classes, Izzy thought, *My friends are right. I may stink at Forensics, but I sting on the ice. At least ...* She took a shaky breath, *I will if my secret works!*

2

On their way to their lockers after their last classes
of the day, Izzy, Allie, and Charlie bumped into the
principal of Atom Middle School, Mr. Delmonico.

"Just the girls I wanted to see," said Mr. Delmonico.
"About that STEM team you want: The school board has
approved the idea of it but has allotted less than the total
amount of money necessary. In fact, they've approved
only half of the needed funds. You'll have to raise the
other half on your own in order to proceed."

Allie piped up immediately, "We'll sell refreshments
at the pop-up science fair," she said impulsively. "The
money we raise can help fund the team."

"Uh, Allie?" Izzy began. "Wait, we—"

But Mr. Delmonico, heading off to coach basketball

practice, was already hurrying away toward the gym. "Good idea," he called back over his shoulder as he disappeared down the hall.

"Jeesh, Allie," fretted Izzy. "Talk about overload. We haven't even decided on our project yet, much less started it. And now you've promised we'll make food for the science fair, too. How're we supposed to pull all this off in ten days?"

Charlie nodded. "Izzy's right, Al," she said. "You should have asked us before you told the principal."

"It'll be easy-peasy," Allie said with a dismissive wave. "We'll use my Bubbie's recipe for chocolate chip cookies and sell a million of them."

"Your grandmother's cookies are The Best," Izzy had to admit.

"Delicious," agreed Charlie.

"But, still," said Izzy.

"But nothing," said Allie. "Don't warp speed into worrywart mode like you usually do, Dizzy Izzy. Chill."

"Ohhh-kaaay," sighed Izzy, unconvinced.

By now, the girls had reached their lockers. Izzy tugged her bulky hockey bag out and slung it over her

shoulder. The bag was so heavy that she lost her balance and started to topple backward.

"Steady," said Charlie, catching her.

"That bag is as big as you are," said Allie. "I bet it weighs just about as much, too."

"Yup!" said Izzy. "It's weird: The equipment's heavy, but when I'm skating, I feel weightless."

"Okay, Ms. Hockey Stick," joked Allie.

"Good luck with the puck!" added Charlie.

"Thanks," said Izzy. She headed out of the school, across the playground, and down the hill. Atom Middle School didn't have an ice rink, but the nearby community center did. Izzy was grateful it was close, because not only was her bag super heavy but it had also started to drizzle. Izzy bent forward to shield her face from the rain as she hurried the short distance to the rink.

As soon as the door swung open, Izzy was greeted by the familiar odor of chlorine from the pool, coffee from the snack bar, and gym socks from the locker rooms.

"Izzy," said Ralph, the man behind the desk. "Good to see you. You're here for tryouts, right?"

"Right," Izzy nodded, shaking raindrops off her hair.

"You've practiced hard," said Ralph. He gave her a thumbs-up. "Now go get 'em."

"Thanks, Ralph," said Izzy, grinning.

Ralph knew that every weekday morning all summer, Izzy and her brothers, Joseph and Lucas, had come to the community center to skate. Joseph was 15 and Lucas was 14. They were counselors at the summer day camp, but before their campers arrived, they practiced ice hockey with Izzy. It had been tough to find a time that the rink was free because it was in use practically 24 hours a day. Several high school teams used it, adult leagues met there, and while wobbly little kids had skating lessons on the edges, figure skaters waltzed, spun, leapt, and perfected their routines in the center of the ice.

Izzy had never been on a hockey team, but she loved the game. Practically as soon as she could walk, her brothers had suited her up with their outgrown hockey equipment and an old wooden goaltender's stick. It was slightly wider and less angled than a regular stick and curved toward the direction of play. At first, all Joseph and Lucas wanted Izzy to do was to be their goalie. Her job was to stand in the goal and block the shots they tried to sneak past her into the net. But as Izzy got older and faster on her skates, she and her brothers began taking turns as goalie so that Izzy could take shots, too. Lucas gave her his regulation stick when he outgrew it. This summer, Izzy had perfected her power turns, crossovers, speed starts, sprints, and—really important—how to fall and get back up quickly.

Even after all the summer mornings of practice, Izzy's hands shook with nervous excitement as she put on her hockey gear now. She had been waiting for this day for a long time: This was the day she'd try out for and—she hoped—make the team. This was the day she might finally spring her surprise.

Izzy was by herself in the Girls' Locker Room strapping on her shin guards when a group of girls arrived. Izzy recognized them as figure skaters.

"What are you doing?" asked one girl. Izzy knew that her name was Maddie Sharpe, because even though Izzy was only a sixth grader, she was in Maddie's eighth grade math class. Maddie frowned and looked at Izzy sideways. "Are you like, getting prepped for ice hockey?"

"Wait, you're that little sixth grader who talked about starting a STEM team on sign-up day, aren't you?" asked a tall girl Izzy didn't know.

Izzy nodded.

"My brother wrote his name on your list," the tall girl

went on. "He says the team's a flop so far; it doesn't even exist yet. I guess that STEM stuff isn't working out too well for you."

Maddie Sharpe waved her hand at Izzy's gear, "This isn't going to work, either," she said. "Girls don't play ice hockey."

Izzy popped her mouth guard out just long enough to say, "I do."

"Eww," squealed the tall girl as Izzy popped the mouth guard, which looked like a giant set of black false teeth, back into her mouth and smiled. Some of the other girls snickered.

Izzy knew that she looked pretty funny in her hockey gear. Her skates were beat-up and clunky. Her knee guards looked like deflated soccer balls. Her black shorts were so humongous that she pulled them up into her armpits, which made her hockey jersey stick out as if her chest were inflated. And she hadn't even added her shoulder guards, neck guard, wristbands, helmet, or gloves yet.

"Listen," said Maddie. "There's no way you're going to make the team. Trust me. First of all, you're a girl. Second, you're a sixth grader. And third, no offense, but you're a shrimp. Those ice hockey guys are gigantic. You'll be crushed like a bug."

"Pushed and squooshed," joked the tall girl.

Izzy shrugged, as if to say, *Maybe*.

"Okay, go ahead," said Maddie, shaking her head and gesturing toward the door that led to the ice rink. "Don't say we didn't warn you."

"You'll see," said another girl in a singsongy voice.

We'll see who'll see, Izzy sang back silently. As she put on her face mask and helmet, she talked to the girls in her head: *First of all, my brothers taught me everything I need to know for today. Second, the S.M.A.R.T. Squad is sure I can do it. Third, no offense, but you obviously don't understand anything about ice hockey or physics. Being small isn't a flaw. It's an advantage. And fourth, well, I've got a secret that'll change everything.*

Still, she sighed. Maddie and her friends thought that she was a dork for suggesting the STEM team, a flop because the STEM team was a no go, a weirdo for wanting to play ice hockey, and a loser who'd never make the team. *It's not that I want to fit in with Maddie and her friends,* Izzy thought. *But oh, man. Middle school is going to be a slog if over and over again, you run smack into snark from people like Maddie Sharpe and you have to decide, Do I do what I want to do, or do I cave?*

Izzy waddled out to the rink, sat on the bench with the other hockey players, and laced up her skates. They were black, beaten-up, broken-in hand-me-downs from her brothers, but Izzy loved them. They had good karma. Lucas's old stick did, too. She pulled on her gloves, which were also pass-alongs. A kid down the bench leaned forward and waved to her. It was Trevor, from her math class. Izzy was a little surprised that Trevor had recognized her even with her helmet and face mask on. She waved back, her giant glove looking like the World's Largest Oven Mitt.

"Okay, guys," ordered Coach Peck. He tossed everyone a numbered jersey. "Put your jersey on and remember your number. I don't know anybody's name yet, so if you hear me shout your number, I'm shouting at you. Onto the ice now. Hustle."

Izzy's jersey number was 12. She was relieved to see that when everyone was suited up they were all alike, except for their sizes and jersey numbers, and everyone looked as nervous as she felt.

Everybody fell a lot, including Izzy. Though because she was short her center of gravity was low, which helped her keep her balance. And when she did fall, another advantage of being short was that she could get up again really quickly. She was nimble, even in all her heavy equipment. Some of the kids hugged the boards and tried not to fall, but Coach Peck waved them out onto the ice.

"Gotta learn how to fall and not get hurt," he said. "And not get run over."

Bam! Oof! Izzy got the wind knocked out of her when all at once three players, looking like a six-legged-hockey monster, fell into her and slammed her against

the plexiglass window so hard that her arm went numb for a second. But she shook them off and chased the puck as it skittered back into the center of the rink.

Coach Peck also had them do one of Izzy's favorite drills. The players lined up across the ice. Izzy dug the toe of her skate into the ice and … *Breeet!* When Coach Peck blew his whistle, she used all her energy and strength to push off as hard as she could in a power start. It was again an advantage to be small; she had less inertia to overcome than the bigger kids did, and less weight to propel. When they hit top speed, the players threw themselves down face-first on the ice and *s-l-i-d*. Izzy careened across the ice on her stomach like a penguin—a super fast, compact penguin, because she didn't have long legs dragging behind her slowing her down.

"Hey, 12, nice slide!" Coach Peck hollered at Izzy. "Good effort."

After the drill, Coach Peck broke them into two groups and had them scrimmage. Izzy thought Coach Peck might be surprised to know that her love of physics helped her be a good ice hockey player. She knew force equals mass multiplied by acceleration. That was

Newton's Second Law of Motion. And she also knew that since she was small, she clearly would never have the most mass. So, she had to have extra acceleration to be a force on the ice. She had trained herself to be *fast*. But being fast wasn't enough. During the scrimmage, Izzy showed Coach Peck that because she was little, she could squeeze between players, slip around them, and slide through narrow gaps.

And on top of *that*—Izzy heard a drumroll in her head—she had

her Cosmic Secret,

her Trick Shot,

her Sure Thing:

The Skidizzy!

The Skidizzy was a special shot that Izzy had invented and her brothers had named. All summer, every morning when she and her brothers went to the rink, Izzy had worked hard to perfect her trick shot. Over and over and over again, Izzy did The Skidizzy. Now, in the scrimmage, Izzy patiently bided her time. She didn't want to blow it by shooting too soon. She waited for the perfect moment to try it.

At last, the moment came.

Izzy bent low to the ice, stole the puck from the kid who was dribbling it, slipped between two defenders, and *wham!* She shot The Skidizzy. The trick was that she hit the ice just *behind* the puck, which made her hockey stick bow. When the stick hit the puck, the stick snapped back into place, releasing energy into the puck. Izzy did a slight flick of the wrists at the end of the motion, which spun the puck so that it sailed through the air in a stable trajectory, making the shot accurate. *Bam!* Into the net.

For a split second, everyone froze and stared at Izzy, even Coach Peck. Izzy was elated: Springing her surprise, making the shot, doing The Skidizzy in a game, even though it was only a tryout scrimmage, had been even cooler than she'd imagined. It was stupendous. Izzy smiled with quiet satisfaction. *Hey, figure skaters,* she thought. *Did you see that?*

Suddenly, everyone came to life. Her teammates raised their sticks and cheered for her, and from the stands, Izzy heard familiar voices shouting, "Izz-ee! Izz-ee! Izz-ee!" She looked up and saw Allie, Charlie, and Gina: her own private cheering squad who'd come to surprise her. Her friends jumped up and down, yelling and waving to her. Izzy waved back to them, and they cheered even louder.

Brreet! Brreet! Brreet! Coach Peck's whistle shrilled. "That's it for today," he said. "Hit the lockers. Team roster will be posted tomorrow. Thanks for coming out, everyone."

Izzy's friends were waiting for her in the locker room. They circled her in a group hug and bounced, saying, "Way to go, Izzy!"

"*Brava,* Izzy. Gina and I finished our sprints early to

come watch you," said Charlie. "And I'm glad we did. That shot of yours was a-maaaa-zing."

"Unbelievably fast!" said Gina, swooping her arm through the air.

"I'll say," agreed Charlie. "Blink and you miss it."

"That's The Skidizzy," said Izzy. "I practiced it all summer in secret."

"You sneak," said Allie, whapping her playfully on her helmet. "Outstanding name: The Skidizzy!"

"You're a jock *and* a science nerd," said Gina. "That is ridiculously rad."

"Did you make the team?" asked Allie.

"Dunno yet," shrugged Izzy. She tried to cross her fingers but her hockey gloves were too stiff.

"You will," said Charlie. "You were a star out there, a shooting star!"

"Well, hurry up and change, Ms. Skidizzy," said Allie. "We'll wait in the library."

Her friends left. As she took off her equipment, Izzy remembered how bummed out she'd been by Maddie Sharpe's snarkiness. *But I was wrong,* she thought happily. *Middle school is totally fine if you have a circle of friends who are—as Gina would say—ridiculously rad, like I do.*

3

The drizzle had morphed into heavy rain by the time Izzy left the community center and crossed the parking lot on her way back to the school building. She was hunched over, trying to keep her face dry, when she heard Coach Peck call out, "Hey, Number 12, right? What's your name again?"

Izzy was so surprised that she stammered, "Iz-zizzy Newton."

"Well, Newton, I've never had a girl on the team," said Coach Peck. He stood next to his car, arms crossed. "And never such a small player, either."

Izzy's heart felt as heavy as her hockey bag. It sank to her shoes.

Then Coach Peck said, "I think it might be good.

Can you keep up that hustle you showed today?"

"Yes," Izzy promised. No stammer this time.

"All right, then," said Coach Peck. "See you at team practice."

"Yes, sir," Izzy glowed. *She'd made the team!* She was so pumped that she was surprised she didn't rise right up off the ground. "Thanks, Coach."

Coach Peck waved and got into his car.

Trevor, unlocking his bike from the bike stand, had overheard. "Congratulations on making the team, Izzy," he said. "It's no wonder. You're a gravitational wave on the ice."

"Thanks," said Izzy. She knew that a gravitational wave was so fast that it made ripples in space-time, like a boat causes ripples in a pond. "I hope you make it."

"Me too," said Trevor. "And I also hope you'll

38

teach me that trick shot of yours."

"The Skidizzy," said Izzy.

Trevor laughed. "Good name," he said. "So you'll teach me how to do it. Deal?"

"Deal," said Izzy, swiping a big raindrop off the end of her nose.

"Over here, Izzy," Allie called impatiently. She waved a white tissue to catch Izzy's eye and beckon her over to the table in the library where the girls were gathered. Izzy might be fast on the ice, but no one was ever quick enough when Allie was waiting. Allie sneezed into the tissue, and her white blond hair stood out from her head in a static fringe. "We've been waiting forever," she complained. But "forever" sounded like "for-ebber" because her nose was clogged.

Izzy slipped into the last chair at the table, which was by the window. She was glad the table was tucked into a corner of the library that was so shaded that it felt cool. After an usually cold September, October had been stuffy: hot, humid, steamy, and rainy. Plus, Izzy was still overheated and sweaty from ice hockey practice, and tired, too. But she was also exhilarated.

Charlie squinted at her. "I can tell by your face and your body language that you've had good news," she said. "You're like the human equivalent of fireworks. You made the team, didn't you?"

Izzy nodded. She couldn't suppress a smile a mile wide. She felt fizzy, like she was full of bubbly ginger ale.

Making the team was a dream come true.

"Yes!" cheered Charlie.

"Game *on*," said Gina. "I can't wait to see you make that Skidizzy shot again. It is *epic*."

This time, Izzy knew that Gina was saying exactly what she meant and not the opposite.

"I bet your picture will be in the school newspaper," gushed Allie, her blue eyes bright with excitement. "You'll be famous: the first ever girl on the hockey team. And not just *on* the team, but the *star* of the team." She paused to blow her nose.

"Oh, no," said Izzy modestly, though she secretly hoped she would be.

"Now," said Allie, briskly, getting down to business. "I've already done some research, and I think the best science fair project for us is my idea of a traffic study. We can film the buses and do a time-motion study about getting to class in the morning without being tardy. First—"

"Hey," Gina interrupted, "don't you hate that dream where you're late to class and you're moving in slo-mo, and no matter how hard you try, you can't move faster?"

"Yes," said Izzy. "Nightmare."

"And sometimes, you're lost and can't find the classroom," Charlie chimed in.

"Right," said Gina. "And you're like, 'I'm roasted.'"

"Okay," said Allie. "Enough with the dream talk. We all agree that this is a great project. We'll use my laptop to film all the kids getting here in the morning on the buses or bikes or on foot or whatever, and then we'll come up with a plan to make it all go faster so kids get to class on time."

"The problem is not just morning arrivals," said Gina. Her nose was runny. She pulled a big bandana out of her backpack and wiped it. "I hate it when teachers keep us in the classroom after the bell rings, and then we get blasted for being late to our next class. It's not our fault we're late. The teachers don't give us enough time to fight our way through the halls, which are jammed."

"I know," said Izzy and Charlie indignantly.

"And how dumb is it that the punishment for being late is less free time after lunch?" said Charlie. "Sometimes that's our only chance to go outside. It's been so rainy that the track team has even had to practice inside, running up and down the stairs and in the halls because the basketball team is using the gym. What a pain in the neck!" She rubbed her head and neck, as if they really were causing her pain.

"Maybe we could do behavior modification therapy for the teachers," said Gina. She took off her glasses and used a dry corner of her bandana to wipe them and then dab her eyes, which were sort of red. "I could compose a musical warning to play over the PA system to let the teachers know the bell's going to ring in two minutes."

"Like the two-minute warning signal in football," said Charlie.

"And then when the bell rings, someone on the intercom would say, 'All rise.' You know, like they do on TV when the judge comes into the courtroom," suggested Izzy. "And we'd all get up and go. That way—"

"Let's focus," interrupted Allie, holding her hands palm up. "Gina, your idea and my idea are both about saving time. I think we can combine them."

"How?" asked Gina.

"Well, of course, first we'll do my idea of the stop-action film of the buses arriving and figure out how to

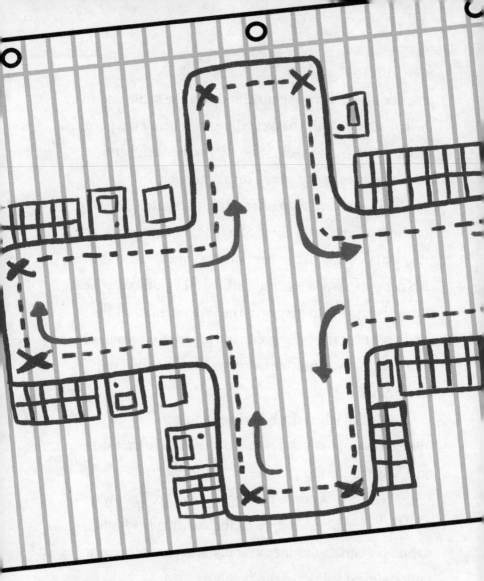

make that more efficient. And then, uh, well, let's see," said Allie. Suddenly, she flapped her hands, "Got it!" She pulled a sheet of paper out of her notebook and drew a sketch.

"See? We'll paint a circuit walk on the hallway floors. Everyone has to hug the wall to their left and not crisscross or jaywalk mid-hall, even to get to their lockers or a classroom door."

"Okay, but what if you want to change directions?" asked Charlie.

"You'll change directions only at designated spots," said Allie. "They'll be at the bottom of the circuit, which would be at the end of a hallway." Allie marked the turnarounds on her sketch with X's. "That way there'll be no collisions."

"Well, that does sound good, Allie," said Izzy. "But hit your pause button. Before we keep going, we'd better make sure everyone agrees, and Marie isn't here. We should ask her if she's cool with the whole idea of a traffic-pattern science fair project." Izzy paused, then punned, "We need her to give it the green light."

"Yeah. I'm not sure Marie will like it," said Gina.

"Why not?" asked Allie, sounding right on the edge of being miffed.

"Well, you like it—it's right up your alley, Allie—because it has lots of math in it," explained Izzy, "like circuits and numbers of buses and students and minutes and distances. But Marie's more into chemistry. You know, like mixing up smelly solutions in beakers and stuff."

"Oh, Marie will go for my plan," said Allie confidently. "Trust me; she'll be all over it."

Izzy cleared her throat. It felt a little tight and itchy, maybe from the uncomfortable feeling that headstrong Allie was wrong to just breezily assume that Marie would like her project without even asking her. Izzy met Charlie's glance; they both knew that Marie and Allie were impatient with each other sometimes. Allie drove Marie crazy with her "the more the merrier" enthusiasm and her "full speed ahead" bossiness. And Marie drove Allie crazy with how fussy and finicky she could be. Izzy swallowed hard, not knowing what to say, and not wanting to make the hairline fracture between Allie and Marie any bigger.

Fortunately, at that moment, Allie let loose a whopper "Ahh-*chooooooo!*"

Ms. Okeke, the librarian, came over to their table. "Hello, girls," said Ms. Okeke. Her voice sounded nasal because she also had a stuffy nose. She handed Allie a box of tissues. "Help yourself."

"Thanks," said Allie. She dabbed her red-rimmed eyes and blew her nose.

Ms. Okeke sighed, but it turned into a cough. "I'm sniffly, too," she rasped. "Lately, it seems like everyone who comes to the library is attacked by upper respiratory congestion."

Izzy sat up straight, listening carefully. She sensed a mystery.

"Now that you mention it, my eyes and nose have been runny ever since I came in here this afternoon," said Gina.

"My throat is itchy, too," said Izzy hoarsely.

"I have sort of a headache," Charlie admitted.

Allie didn't say anything, but she blew her nose again, with a loud honk.

"What is going on?" asked Charlie. "What's giving everyone these weird symptoms?"

"It's a puzzle," said Ms. Okeke, "and if someone could

47

solve it, I'd be grateful."

Ms. Okeke left, and Gina, Izzy, and Charlie exchanged excited, delighted grins.

"Are you thinking what I'm thinking?" asked Izzy. She rhymed the syllables, "The Li-brar-ee Mys-ter-ee. Has a nice ring to it, right? Sure does sound like a job for the S.M.A.R.T. Squad."

"Do you get the feeling that Ms. Okeke is on to us?" asked Allie.

"What do you mean?" asked Charlie.

"I think she suspects that we're the ones who solved The Mystery of the Cold School," said Allie, "and that's why she pretty much just asked us to solve The Library Mystery. But do we want to?"

"You mean because it might be dangerous?" asked Charlie. "Because whatever is making people sick might make us sick, too?"

"No," said Allie.

"Then why wouldn't we want to figure it out?" asked Izzy.

"Because, duh," Allie puffed impatiently. "We have to focus on our science fair project, of course. You got all bent out of shape when I told Mr. Delmonico we'd make and sell refreshments at the science fair because you thought that was too much on top of our project. Now you want to tackle this library thingy, too? There's no way we can do all that." She held her forehead, shaking her head. "And you guys think *I'm* the one who piles on!"

Izzy texted Marie that night to tell her that the Squad was going to meet before school the next day. It was raining again, so they had to meet in the little room that led to the roof. Izzy could hear the rain pattering on the skylight. It was gloomy until Gina turned on the soft-glow desk lamps she'd brought from home. Back in September, when the girls first found this little space, it had been dusty and full of old boxes. They had cleaned it out and furnished it with a rug and big floor pillows to sit on. They used upside-down boxes as tables, and Charlie had provided a cooler that she kept stocked with apples.

"What's up?" asked Marie as she flopped down onto a red pillow.

"Your collar, for one thing," said Allie. "It's standing up all around your neck." She wiggled her fingers around her own neck. "Fold it down."

Izzy saw a flicker of annoyance cross Marie's face.

"No," Marie said to Allie. "I want my collar up. It's the preppy look."

"Oh," said Allie, raising her eyebrows and taking a step back.

Uh-oh, Izzy winced. *Here we go.* She knew that Marie and Allie were polar opposites when it came to fashion. Marie was very particular about her appearance. It was important to her to be up-to-the-minute hip. Today, for example, Izzy could see that Marie had changed the streak in her hair from the green that it had been yesterday to pink, to go with her pink socks. Izzy knew that Allie, on the other hand, cheerfully wore blue every day; she had to, because she'd carelessly washed her shirts with her new blue jeggings and the color had run. Quickly, before Marie and Allie started fashion bashing each other, Izzy jumped in to defuse the tension. "Your collar looks very cool," she said to Marie.

Marie softened at the compliment.

"Hey, see this?" Izzy continued. She held up a black-and-white composition book, just like the one the Squad had used when they solved The Mystery of the Cold School. "New book, new mystery," she said. "The S.M.A.R.T. Squad has a new project."

"A new mystery?" said Marie. "Spill."

"Get this," said Charlie. "Something weird is going on in the library. It's a plague. Ms. Okeke told us that everybody's sneezing and sniffling in there and getting runny noses and red eyes."

"And WE are going to figure out why," said Gina.

"The symptoms sound like allergic reactions," said Charlie.

Marie's eyes lit up. Immediately, she said, "Chemicals used to clean the rugs could cause allergic reactions. Or maybe it's the plants in the library. Lots of people are allergic to plants. Or maybe the cafeteria vents into the library, and airborne particles of stuff people are allergic to, like peanuts, are floating in."

"You're a genius, Murreee," said Charlie, using Marie's elementary school nickname. "You've given us three good hypotheses right off the top of your head. Your ideas are popping like popcorn. I can't wait to test them."

"Time-out," said Izzy. She held her hands up in a T and made a face of mock dismay. "Did I hear the word 'vent'? Don't tell me I'm going to have to slither through vents again. Last time we solved a mystery, I did that and bumped into a swarm of honeybees. That was a sticky situation, beeee-lieve me."

"*Arrggh,*" moaned Allie. "Again, with the bee jokes. Truly cringe-inducing. They're worse than the bees were."

"Don't worry, Izzy," said Gina. "We all remember how brave you were when you squeezed into the overhead air vents to rescue Teddy-the-robot. Poor guy got stuck when we sent him in to see if blocked vents were causing the problem of the cold school. Snaps to you, Iz, for pulling Teddy and the bees out. I mean, luckily, the bees were nearly frozen, so they were barely moving. But still."

"That hypothesis about the vents was a flop," said Charlie. "But you'll be glad to know that the swarm you saved is thriving in my moms' hives."

"Hives?" repeated Marie enthusiastically. "I wonder if

anyone in the library is breaking out in hives? That's an allergic reaction, too. I knew a kid who was so allergic to peanuts that he broke out in hives from touching a table where somebody had eaten peanuts. The plot of The Library Mystery thickens. Let's get going on it."

"Cool your jets," said Allie with a laugh, but she clearly wasn't joking. "We're slamming the breaks on my science fair project about fixing traffic to get to class on time?"

"Oh, no," said Izzy. She made a pun hoping to help Allie lighten up. "We're just temporarily shelving it for the library job. Don't worry. We can do both."

"Sure," said Gina confidently. "Congested halls, congested noses. The Library Mystery is no problem for the S.M.A.R.T. Squad."

Allie looked peeved and unconvinced. "Okay, I'm just going to remind you that the science fair is next week," she said. "And don't forget that we also have to make cookies to sell to raise money for the STEM team."

Charlie soothed her. "Sure, Al," she said. "We know. Don't worry. We'll save a day to do your traffic idea and make cookies to sell."

"Say what now?" asked Marie sharply. "Our science fair project is about cookies and traffic? You all decided that yesterday without me?"

"Well," Gina began. "We—"

"I mean because I think traffic is boring," Marie cut in. "I want to do something exciting. Something that has to do with chemical reactions like combustion or decomposition or redox."

"Something loud or smelly?" snorted Allie. "Like an explosion?"

"Yes, exactly," said Marie.

"Wicked," said Gina approvingly.

"I don't get it, Marie," said Allie. "You hate dirt and gunk, but you love smelly chemical solutions?"

"Traffic just seems like talking to me," said Marie. "What would we show at the science fair: charts? What a yawn. My sister said that in sixth grade she made a volcano."

"Oh, please," groaned Allie. "Everyone does that."

"Because it's fun," said Marie crossly. "And we could do something *super* new and *super* cool, like add phosphorescent paint to the chemicals so that when the volcano explodes—"

"It'll be *super* lame," Allie interrupted.

It seemed to Izzy that the fissure between Allie and Marie was widening into an abyss. "Listen," she said. "I think we're lucky that we have two good ideas. Right now, the library plague is a crisis. It's going to take ALL of us using ALL our smarts. Let's focus on that mystery first. Then we can decide whether or not we're doing a volcano or traffic or something else for the science fair."

Under her breath, Marie honked like a car horn, "Beep, beep." She rolled her eyes to show exaggerated boredom at the traffic idea. But luckily, Allie didn't see or hear her because the alarm on Allie's watch beeped, which meant it was time to hurry off to morning classes.

"Hey."

Izzy felt Trevor poke her in the back. She was at her locker, before her first class. "Hey, what?" she asked.

"The hockey team list is posted," said Trevor. "You

made the cut, as we already know."

"Oh! Did you make the team, too?" Izzy asked.

"Yeah, but I'm a sub," said Trevor. "I may not get to play, but I'll practice with the team and suit up for the games."

"Cool," said Izzy.

"And," said Trevor. "When you teach me that secret shot of yours, The Skidizzy, I bet I get promoted to first string."

"Sure," said Izzy.

As she went down the hall, Izzy was so happy that she felt as if she were flying. Unfortunately, her first class of the day was Forensics and sure enough, there she crashed and burned.

It was the worst of the worst assignments: The teacher, Ms. Martinez, called students to the front of the room to speak for two minutes "extemporaneously" on a surprise topic. That was like a pop quiz, Forensics-style. As her classmates spoke, Izzy tried hard to be invisible. Her heart sank when Ms. Martinez looked straight at her and said, "Izzy, tell us about your favorite sport."

Okay, I can do this, Izzy thought as she walked to the

front of the room on boneless legs. *I could talk about ice hockey for two hours. Two minutes will be a breeze. Right?* She took such a deep breath that her chest stuck out. When she spoke, she was horrified to hear herself say in a voice that warbled, "Ice hockey is my spavorite fort."

A big guy in the front row burst out laughing. Instantly, the laughter spread like a contagious rash, and soon the whole room was howling. Even though they didn't sound mean, Izzy froze. She felt hot, then cold, then faint, and so miserable that she could not manage to say another word. She felt totally embarrassed. The clock ticked agonizingly slowly. The class waited. Their laughter fizzled out until they weren't laughing at all anymore, just shuffling uncomfortably in their seats. Still, Izzy could not talk. Talk? Ha! She could hardly breathe. Finally, Ms. Martinez took pity on Izzy and let her sit down. "See me after class, Izzy," she said.

When class was finally over, everyone left. No one looked at Izzy as they filed out.

Ms. Martinez sat next to Izzy and sighed.

Izzy sighed, too. She bit her lip, put her chin on her fists, and stared down at her desk.

"Okay, Izzy." Ms. Martinez sounded kind but firm. "Explain."

Izzy took a deep, shuddering breath. "I can't help it," she wailed. "I just cannot talk in front of people. It's a personality flaw. The other kids are lucky. It's easy for them to stand up and make a speech."

"Lucky? I don't know about that," said Ms. Martinez. "My favorite poet, Emily Dickinson, says 'Luck is not chance—it's toil. Fortune's expensive smile is earned.'"

"I'll work," said Izzy. "Could I write something and hand it out to everybody? Or record a speech and play that? Or make a speech only to you?"

"No," said Ms. Martinez. "The purpose of Forensics is to learn public speaking. That means speaking in front of a group. There's no negotiating. If you don't speak, you won't pass. I can't bend the rules for you." She sighed. "I know it's hard. But you've got to try. Write a speech on the topic of 'My Greatest Challenge.' Go over it and over it until you've got it by heart. It'll help if you practice at home and with your friends. Then when I ask you to present it in class, I expect you to stand up, speak up, and be heard. Okay?"

"Okay," said Izzy, even though she knew it was not okay, and never would be.

Izzy was silent during her next class, which was History. At lunch, she felt so queasy about Forensics that she couldn't eat. The cafeteria smelled like old baloney anyway, and the students' voices were ear-splittingly loud. They shouted across the long tables at one another. Even in all that cacophony, Izzy could have sworn she heard someone say "spavorite fort" to a table that then combusted into laughter. One girl laughed so hard she fell off her chair. Izzy crammed her uneaten tuna sandwich back into her lunch bag, balled up the bag, and tossed it in the trash.

"What's the matter?" asked Charlie, who was devotedly devouring a salad in a bowl as big as a basin. "Did you bomb in Forensics again?"

"Big-time," Izzy nodded. "A one-hundred percent panic attack freeze-up. This time, I couldn't even get my mouth to work right. I called hockey my spavorite fort, and everybody laughed. I felt like a loser. And let's face it: I was. Jumbotron size."

"Ouch, that's harsh," said Marie.

"Look at it this way," said Allie, waggling her half-eaten apple. "At least you gave your classmates a laugh for the day. There are worse things than that, right? I myself love to make people laugh."

"Next time, Izzy," suggested Charlie, "remember to breathe. And it might help to hold something in your hand, like a pencil, and pretend to squeeze all your anxiety into it."

"When I play my violin, I close my eyes if I'm nervous," said Allie. "Works every time."

"What do you do when you play your flute in front of people, Izzy?" asked Marie.

"I never do," said Izzy.

"Oh," said Marie.

"Just be yourself when you make your speech," said Gina simply.

"No, don't," said Allie. "Whatever you do, don't just be yourself. I know everyone always says that, but in your case, Izzy, I don't think it's good advice. Look where it's gotten you so far: exactly nowhere."

Even though it was hard to hear, Izzy thought Allie was probably right. She was grateful to her friends, but as they gave their advice, she was thinking, *Easy for you to say.* None of them were in Forensics. It was excruciating to be a dud, and embarrassing to talk about it.

Izzy was glad that the girls ate fast and then divvied up Marie's three hypotheses about why people were sneezing in the library. Izzy and Marie teamed up, and so did Allie and Gina. Charlie was going solo. They decided to use the rest of their lunch period to investigate the hypotheses and then meet after their clubs and sports practices to review their findings. *Thank goodness for the S.M.A.R.T. Squad,* Izzy thought. *And thank goodness for ice hockey. Ice hockey is The Best.*

Practice after school that day was intense, which Izzy loved. Her speed and skills were as sharp as her skate blades. She had no trouble keeping up with the rest of the team or following Coach Peck's quick calls or drills. She was even kind of a little bit famous as the inventor of The Skidizzy. The whole team went crazy cheering whenever she made the shot.

"All the guys are psyched for our first game," said Trevor when Izzy was resting on the bench between drills. "You're going to wow the other team with your phenomenal shot, The—unstoppable, tricky, 'now you see it now you don't'—Skidizzy."

"When's the first game?" Izzy asked.

"Not until a week from Saturday," said Trevor, "after report cards come out."

Izzy tensed at the mention of report cards. But she had no time or energy to waste on worry. Coach Peck meant business. Practice took all of Izzy's attention.

By the time practice was over and Izzy was on her way to meet with her friends, she'd practically forgotten about both report cards and her horrendous humiliation in Forensics. Whenever thoughts of either one tried to slide into her mind, she'd whack 'em away as hard and fast and far as she'd whacked the hockey puck.

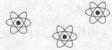

"I sure hope that one of my hypotheses is right," said Marie as Izzy took the black-and-white composition book out of her backpack. They were sitting on the floor pillows, waiting for the other girls to join them in the little room that led to the roof and report back about their investigations.

"It's too bad our investigation of the carpet cleaner hypothesis failed," said Izzy. "But I bet one of your other two hypotheses is right." She joked, "Chemists like you always have the right solutions. Get it?"

Marie groaned and rolled her eyes at Izzy's wince-worthy pun, but Izzy could tell that she was pleased.

When all the girls were gathered, Izzy held the composition book open. "Here's what Marie and I found out," she said. "Spoiler alert: The carpet cleaner hypothesis was a washout." She showed the other girls what she had written.

S.M.A.R.T. SQUAD

From Izzy and Marie
- Make an Observation: People are sneezing in the library.
- Form a Question: What is causing the irritation?
- Form a Hypothesis: The chemical solvent used to clean the rugs in the library is an irritant.
- Conduct an Experiment: Ask the custodians if the solvent is used in any other rooms, and if people sneeze in those rooms.
- Analyze the Data and Draw a Conclusion: Custodians report that the same solvent is used in lots of rooms— the auditorium, the main office reception area, and the teachers' lounge—and no one has complained about sneezing in any of those places. So, the solvent is NOT the cause.

Allie held out her hand for the book. "Hand it over," she said. "Gina and I have bad news, too. We investigated Marie's idea about air ducts and vents. That hypothesis turned out to be full of hot air."

Gina nodded. "It was a dead end," she said.

68

Allie wrote in the book:

From Allie and Gina

- Make an Observation: People are sneezing in the library.

- Form a Question: What is causing the irritation?

- Form a Hypothesis: Air ducts from the cafeteria send food particles and odors through vents into the library.

- Conduct an Experiment: Check out the duct system— again. This time, study the diagram of the system that Allie downloaded to her laptop.

- Analyze the Data and Draw a Conclusion: There are no ducts connected to the cafeteria that could send food particles or odors through vents into the library. Therefore, food particles and odors are NOT causing the irritation in the library.

"I'm afraid I came up with *nada*, too," said Charlie. "I looked into Marie's hypothesis about plants in the library making people sneeze. But they're not. They couldn't." Charlie wrote:

From Charlie:
- Make an Observation: People are sneezing in the library.
- Form a Question: What is causing the irritation?
- Form a Hypothesis: People are allergic to the plants in the library.
- Conduct an Experiment: Examine and identify the plants.
- Analyze the Data and Draw a Conclusion: All plants in the library are fake. Therefore, plants are NOT causing people to sneeze.

Allie made the sound of an exploding bomb, *Pikooo!* "Well," she said bluntly, "we sure disproved all three of Marie's hypotheses really quickly." She turned to Marie. "Sorry."

Marie shrugged. *"C'est la vie,"* she said. "No biggie."

"It would be funny if it weren't tragic," said Gina.

"Hey," said Izzy. "Don't freak. Remember last time? Our hypotheses about why the school was cold tanked over and over again until we finally hit it right."

"You mean 'lit' it right," joked Charlie, "by swapping out the old incandescent lightbulb for an LED bulb."

"Anybody have any bright ideas now?" asked Marie. "I mean about our new mystery."

"I might," said Charlie.

"Thank goodness," said Allie. "We've got to solve this mystery fast, so we can move on to our science fair project. Tell us, Char."

"Well, when I was in the library checking out the plants, I noticed that one corner—the one where we were sitting before, in fact—smelled kind of rank and dank," said Charlie. "I know it's been raining a lot lately. That's probably why. Do you think a bad smell could make people sneeze and have runny eyes?"

"Sure," said Izzy. "After practice, my hockey socks practically make me faint. I need an oxygen mask to breathe when I'm near them."

"Yuck," said Marie, wrinkling her nose.

"Thanks for sharing that lovely piece of information," joked Allie. "Let's change your name from Isabel Newton to Isa-*smell Pee-yew*-ton. Meanwhile, I think we should go to the library right now, and—"

"Sniff out some clues?" said Izzy.

"Arrggh," moaned Allie. She pinched her nose with her fingers and stuck out her tongue to show how she felt about Izzy's pun.

"Okay, let's go. But be cool," Gina cautioned. She straightened her big-frame glasses. "Remember that our S.M.A.R.T. Squad mystery-solving is secret. No one is supposed to know what we're doing, or why."

The girls hurried to the library. They were relieved to see that the table in the corner was empty. They headed straight toward it.

Gina took a deep breath. "Charlie, you're right," she said. "It smells like something's rotten here."

"What's causing that icky mildew smell?" asked Izzy.

"I have an idea," said Marie. She knelt down, pulled several books off the bookshelf under the window, and peered at the wall behind the shelf. "Yup. I was right," she said. "See that black stuff? That's the problem."

The other girls knelt and looked, too. "What is it?" asked Allie.

Izzy reached forward to touch the black gunk.

"Don't touch it!" said Marie. "It could be dangerous."

5

Izzy jerked back.

"What is it?" Allie asked again.

"That," said Marie, "is mold."

"Sweeeeet," sang Gina, in her full-on, flip-the-meaning mode.

"It's growing on the wall," Marie added.

"Ah," said Charlie. "That makes sense: The rainy, warmer than usual weather we've been having is unfortunately perfect for growing mold."

"So is it dangerous?" asked Gina.

"We don't know what kind of mold it is," explained Marie. "Some molds produce mycotoxins that can make you sick. Others can give you a nasty rash. I'll bring my mold kit to school tomorrow and test this first

thing in the morning."

"You have a mold kit?" asked Izzy. Before Marie could answer, Izzy held up both hands to stop her and went on, "How silly of me. Of course you do. I bet you are the only middle school student in the whole world who has her own mold testing kit." She gave Marie a hug. "You are The Best."

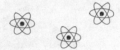

"Hurry up," hissed Gina. It was the next morning, and the girls had gathered in the hall outside the library. Gina opened the door, and Marie gestured frantically for Izzy and Allie to follow her inside.

"Shouldn't we wait for Charlie?" whispered Izzy.

"No," said Gina. "Ms. Okeke will be here soon, not to mention the whole custodial staff. If they see us, we're busted. The secret of the S.M.A.R.T. Squad will be blown."

It was pitch dark in the library, and it smelled so wet that Izzy felt as if she were swimming underwater. Always-prepared Gina flicked on a flashlight and led the way to the corner where Marie had found the mold on the wall behind the books.

"Ahhh-*choooo!*" Allie let a mammoth sneeze rip.

"*Shhhh,*" hissed Izzy and Gina.

The girls crouched around Marie. She was always very careful about following the safety and cleanliness protocols that she'd learned doing chemistry. She took her time to put on goggles, a nose-and-mouth mask, and protective gloves. Gina aimed the flashlight at the wall so Marie could see in the murkiness. Marie opened her mold kit and took out a scalpel, which she used to scrape some mold off the wall and into a petri dish.

Allie whispered a rare compliment, "*Très bien,* Mademoiselle Marie. I've got to say: You are crushing this investigation."

"Copy that," murmured Izzy, "It's like you—"

Suddenly, Izzy was aware of a large shape looming behind her.

"Who's that?" said Gina. She turned swiftly and shined the flashlight in the face of—Charlie.

"Oh, it's only you," Allie breathed in relief. "You scared me."

"Sorry I'm late," said Charlie. She shielded her eyes. "Hey, Gina, could you maybe not blind me with that light? How's it going?"

"Almost done," said Marie. Carefully, she screwed the lid onto the petri dish and stood. "Let's go to the lab and look at this under the microscope."

"Do we have time before everyone gets here and school begins?" asked Gina.

"If we're quick," said Marie.

The girls ran down the dark, echoey hallway from the library to the lab. Once in the lab, still with 15 minutes until school started, Marie peered at the slide, focusing the microscope so that she had a clear view of the sample. "Yup, just as I thought," she said firmly. "This is *Stachybotrys chartarum*, also known as toxic black mold."

"Toxic?" repeated Gina nervously.

"You bet," said Allie. "It's not the smell that's making people's noses run. It's being exposed to this stuff. Listen." She read from her laptop: "Symptoms of black mold poisoning—"

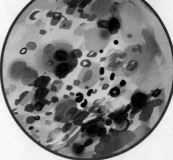

"Poisoning?" interrupted Gina, sounding even more nervous.

Allie read on: "Symptoms of black mold poisoning are similar to symptoms of an upper respiratory tract infection, such as the flu or common cold. For people with asthma, severe attacks can occur. Symptoms caused by exposure to black mold may include headache; sore or itchy throat; stuffy or runny nose; coughing; sneezing; red, itchy, or watery eyes; wheezing; fatigue; and nosebleeds."

"Eww," all the girls said together.

"Bingo," said Allie. "We solved The Library Mystery: Being exposed to mold is making people sick."

"Mold is repulsive," said Izzy, shuddering.

"Well," said Charlie, "In fact, mold is pretty helpful a lot of the time. Like, some molds help create antibiotics. Penicillin is mold. And mold breaks down dead plants and animals and recycles their nutrients back into the ecosystem. Also, we eat some molds."

"No way," said Allie. "Not me."

"You do if you eat mushrooms on your pizza," said Charlie. "Or blue cheese or soy sauce. They've got mold in them."

"Ick," said Gina. "Now I never want to eat anything ever again as long as I live."

"Hey, look," said Izzy. She showed the girls what she had written in the composition book:

- Make an Observation: People are sneezing in the library.
- Form a Question: What is causing the irritation?
- Form a Hypothesis: Mold on the wall behind the books is the irritant.
- Conduct an Experiment: Test the mold.
- Analyze the Data and Draw a Conclusion: The mold is Stachybotrys chartarum, or black mold. Exposure to black mold can cause symptoms of upper respiratory tract infections. Therefore, the cause of the sneezing in the library is mold on the walls behind the books.

"That's good, Izzy," said Charlie, "but solving this mystery has raised—" She thought for a moment, counting on her fingers, then said, "Four new ones. First, how do we get rid of the mold on the walls? Second, can we save the books that have mold on them? Third, where's the mold coming from? And fourth, how can we stop any more mold from growing?"

"Charlotte Roberta Darwin," said Allie. "Bum us out, why don't you? We thought this case was closed. And now you tell us we've got four more mysteries to solve?"

"That's science for you, right?" said Izzy. "Last time, we tried lots of different ways to solve one mystery: The Mystery of the Cold School. This time, one mystery has multiplied into four. The mystery's growing just like the mold."

Gina giggled. She deepened her voice to sound like the narrator of a horror movie and said, "Creepy, crawly monster mold is taking over Atom Middle School."

Charlie picked up the joke. "Where will it appear next?" she intoned. "Locker rooms? The cafeteria? The Girls' Room? Gina Carver's backpack? It's unstoppable."

"It's a rash. It's a sneeze. It's *Stachybotrys chartarum*!"

joked Allie.

"Mold's no joke, you guys," Marie scolded.

"Right. Sorry, Marie," said Gina, coming back to Earth.

"I hear ya, boss," said Izzy. "The question is: Where should we begin our de-molding campaign?"

"I think the most important thing is to stop the immediate problem of people getting sick," said Charlie. "We need to tell Ms. Okeke about the mold right away. I'm sorry to say this, but I think the library will have to be closed."

"But we're—the S.M.AR.T. Squad, I mean—supposed to be a secret, right?" said Gina. "How can we let Ms. Okeke know we've discovered mold and that's why everyone's sneezing, without blowing our cover?"

"I know!" said Allie. She flapped her hands to stop everyone else from talking and, enthusiastically bossy as usual, burst out, "At lunch, we'll sneak into the library. Charlie, you'll be lookout to be sure that no one is watching. Then we'll take the moldy books off the shelf under the window and put them on the table. Meanwhile, Marie, you make a sign with a big arrow. At lunch, we'll leave the arrow sign on the bookshelf, pointing down to the gunky mold on the wall."

"Well," Marie began, "I—"

But Allie steamrolled over her and went on, "And Izzy, you write Ms. Okeke an anonymous letter that tells how mold makes people sniffly and sneezy, and we'll leave that on the table, too. We'll have to act casual. Then no one will suspect us, and our secret identities will remain—" She put her finger to her lips and whispered, "Secret."

"Sounds like a plan," said Charlie. "*Vamonos.*"

"Hold up," said Marie. "Think about it: As soon as Ms. Okeke finds out about the mold, she'll go straight to Mr. Delmonico, and they'll hire professional mold removers who will look for the source of the mold, too. Won't that mean that there's nothing for the S.MA.R.T. Squad to do but watch? Where's the fun in that?"

"Marie is right," said Gina. "We better act fast if we want to solve these mysteries ourselves. Today, after our clubs and practices, we should look for the cause and the source of the mold and suggest a plan to fix it."

Charlie grinned. "S.M.A.R.T. Squad to the rescue."

"And in fast-forward," said Allie, "which is good, because we need to finish up this mold stuff ASAP since we haven't even chosen our science fair project yet. I keep—"

Brrring! Everyone jumped a foot as the bell rang to announce the beginning of the school day.

Saved by the bell, thought Izzy, *from another rant from Allie about the science fair.* Aloud, Izzy said, "Yikes! I was deep into our mystery. I sort of forgot all about school."

"Me too," said Charlie. "Catch you guys later!"

Quickly, the girls shouldered their backpacks, skittered out of the lab, and hurried off to their morning classes.

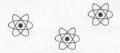

During Study Hall that morning, when she was supposed to be writing the speech for Forensics entitled "My Greatest Challenge," instead, Izzy wrote a note to Ms. Okeke. She printed it in all uppercase letters so that Ms. Okeke wouldn't recognize her handwriting.

DEAR MS. OKEKE,

THE ICKY STUFF YOU SEE ON THE WALLS BEHIND THE BOOKS IN THE LIBRARY IS *STACHYBOTRYS CHARTARUM*, OR BLACK MOLD. WHEN PEOPLE ARE EXPOSED TO BLACK MOLD, THEY MAY SHOW SYMPTOMS SIMILAR TO THOSE OF AN UPPER RESPIRATORY TRACT INFECTION OR A COMMON COLD, WHICH CAN INCLUDE SNEEZING, WHEEZING, COUGHING, STUFFY/RUNNY NOSE, WATERY/RED/ITCHY EYES, SORE/ITCHY THROAT, FATIGUE, AND NOSEBLEEDS. FOR THOSE WITH ASTHMA, EXPOSURE CAN CAUSE AN ATTACK. WE THINK BLACK MOLD IS THE CAUSE OF THE SNEEZING AND SNIFFLING YOU'VE NOTICED LATELY.

SIGNED,
CONCERNED FRIENDS OF THE LIBRARY

Izzy had just finished her note when she realized that, *uh-oh,* the person standing next to her desk was Ms. Martinez. "What's that?" asked Ms. Martinez, looking at Izzy's note.

"Oh," said Izzy. "It's uh, it's—" She went silent.

"Well, I can see what it is not," said Ms. Martinez. "It is not a speech." She tapped Izzy's paper. "Don't you think it would be a good idea to use Study Hall to do your assignment so that you'll be ready for Forensics tomorrow? You're supposed to be writing a speech entitled 'My Greatest Challenge.' And don't forget, you still owe me a speech about your favorite sport."

"Right," Izzy nodded. *I'll write about my greatest challenge first because that will be easy,* she thought. She took a fresh sheet of paper out of her notebook and wrote, My Greatest Challenge: Forensics.

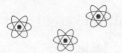

"Yo," said Charlie softly. "Update from the Lookout Department. Good news: It smells so rank in this corner that everyone's steering clear of it."

It was lunchtime. Charlie was standing guard as the S.M.A.R.T. Squad carried out its stealth mission in the library.

Izzy chuckled, and then sneezed. "Yeah," she said. "It's easy to be invisible when there's no one around to see you. Our moldy corner is deserted."

"So far," said Gina nervously, through a stuffed-up nose. "But we better get this over with fast, because someone may show up any second."

Speedily, Marie stuck the arrow sign on the bookshelf so that the arrow pointed to the mold on the wall. Allie and Gina, wearing protective gloves, took moldy books off the shelf and put them on the table. Izzy propped her letter to Ms. Okeke against the pile of books.

"Mission accomplished," said Gina, pulling off her gloves. She pointed her index fingers in opposite directions. "Now scatter, to avoid suspicion."

"You got it," said Marie.

The girls bumped into one another in their hurry to leave the library undetected.

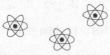

The S.M.A.R.T. Squad was surprised at how quickly things happened after its secret shenanigans. During the last class of the day, which was Spanish for Izzy and Allie, Mr. Delmonico made an announcement over the PA system.

"Atom Middle School students," the principal said, "I regret to inform you that due to a problem with mold, effective immediately, the library is closed until further notice. Students needing to do research are encouraged to go to the public library or to the library at Brassy Intermediate School. Thank you for your cooperation."

Izzy and Allie sneaked glances at each other. Allie grinned and clapped her fingertips, holding her hands close to her chest so that no one but Izzy would notice.

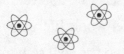

Before ice hockey practice, the boys were buzzing about their upcoming game so much that Coach Peck had to shout for their attention. "Boys!" he shouted. Then he added, "Oh, and Newton. Listen up."

When everyone settled down, Coach Peck said, "Okay, as you know, our first game is a week from next Saturday, against Oaktree Middle School."

Izzy and the boys tapped their hockey sticks against their skates, which was the ice hockey way of showing approval. Coach Peck held up his hands, and when it was quiet, he went on to say, "Report cards come out Monday. If you fail a course, you can't play in any games until you bring that grade up to passing. Work as hard in the classroom as you do on the ice the rest of this week. Go Atomics!"

"Go Atomics!" the team cheered. All except Izzy. She was worried about—what else? Failing Forensics. But then practice started, and in the intensity of skating, Izzy was able to shake off her sense of impending doom. *Chill,* she said to herself. She'd never failed a class or even a pop quiz in her whole life. *Swoosh, bam!* She slammed the puck into the goal so hard it ricocheted off the back. *Take that, Forensics,* she thought.

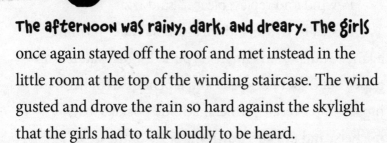

6

The afternoon was rainy, dark, and dreary. The girls once again stayed off the roof and met instead in the little room at the top of the winding staircase. The wind gusted and drove the rain so hard against the skylight that the girls had to talk loudly to be heard.

"I feel like we're on a ship in the middle of the ocean," said Marie.

"In the middle of a storm," added Allie.

"Ahoy, mateys," agreed Izzy.

Gina flicked on the lamps, and their gentle light warmed the room. She took rolled-up blueprints of Atom Middle School out of her overstuffed backpack and spread them on the floor. The girls made themselves cozy. They stretched out on their stomachs, lying on the rug with their chins propped up on pillows so that they could pour over the blueprints.

"The school building is made of bricks and mortar on top of a concrete foundation," said Gina. Her thick eyeglasses reflected the light from the lamps. "And the whole structure is old. My guess is the problem is hydrostatic pressure."

"Rewind and replay, please," said Izzy.

"Basically, hydrostatic pressure is water pushing against walls," said Gina. She pulled some wadded-up paper out of her backpack and a pencil out of her hipster-hip overalls, which had side pockets, back pockets, and pockets down the sides of the legs. "Hang on," said Gina. "I think I can explain it better if I draw it while I talk about it."

Quickly, Gina sketched a comic strip of seven panels. "Old buildings like Atom Middle School shift and settle over the years. Cracks can form in the foundation," said Gina. She added a tiny, jagged line on the foundation to show a crack. "Usually, the water table, or level of water in the ground, stays about the same so there's not much trouble."

"But—" began Charlie.

"But there's big trouble when it rains as much as it has around here lately," said Gina. She moved on to the next panel and drew rain falling from a cloud. "With this much rain, the water table rises because the ground is so saturated that it just can't absorb any more water." She wrote on the cloud: 1. It rains a lot. She drew an arrow in the ground, pointing up, and wrote: 2. The water table rises.

In the third panel, Gina drew big arrows pushing against the foundation, and bigger jagged lines to show bigger cracks. "The wet ground and water push against the foundation, making any cracks bigger and making new cracks, too. Water leaks in through the cracks. Sometimes the ground pushes so hard that it makes walls bow or buckle, or even collapse, like a landslide."

"Bad news," said Allie.

"You got that right," said Gina. She wrote next to the arrows: 3. Water and wet ground push. And next to the cracks, she wrote: 4. Cracks get bigger. New cracks form.

"To add to the trouble, concrete has little holes, or pores, in it, which is why we call it porous," said Gina.

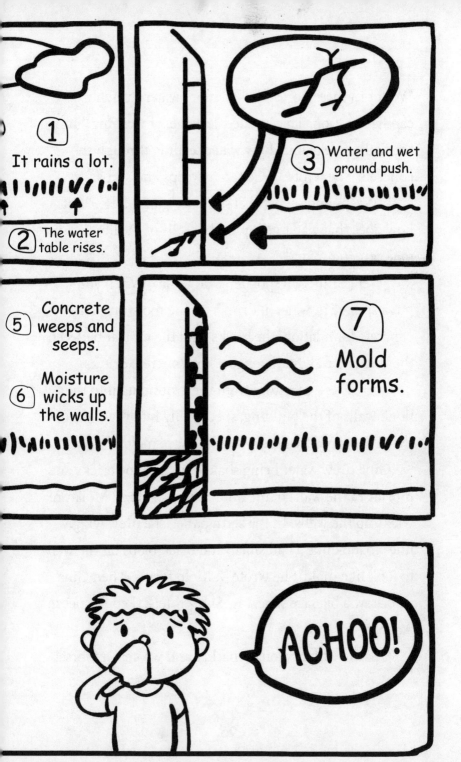

"Water in these pores pulls in more water through capillary action. That's called seepage, or weeping." In the fifth panel, Gina drew water seeping through the concrete. She wrote: 5. Concrete weeps and seeps.

"'Weeps and seeps,' that's poetic," said Marie. "But how does that water get up to the walls of the library and make them moldy?"

"Well, think of a sponge," said Gina. "When you put a sponge in water, it drinks up the moisture. The concrete foundation, the bricks, and the mortar between the bricks are all like sponges. The concrete drinks up—or wicks—moisture from the ground up into the brick walls of the building, specifically into the walls of the library, and that's why the walls are moldy."

Gina drew water being soaked up into the bricks and mortar of the walls of the library. She wrote: 6. Moisture wicks up the walls. In the sixth panel, she drew wiggly lines to look like a bad smell, and black blobs on the wall to look like mold. She wrote: 7. Mold forms. Then Gina just drew a big face sneezing. She wrote: 8. People sneeze. Achoo!

Charlie whipped out a marker and wrote: Or worse!

Quickly, she sketched the poison skull sign with X's for eyes.

"We have to look for a crack in the foundation under the library?" asked Izzy. "Is that what you're saying?"

"Yup," said Gina. "It may be a big crack, or it may be so small that it just looks like a skinny little flaw."

"Speaking of flaws," said Marie, standing and smoothing her skirt. "There's a big one in your plan, Gina: We could get into trouble. We're not exactly allowed to crawl around under the school."

"We're not really supposed to be on the roof, either," said Allie. "But as my Bubbie says, sometimes rules have to be broken."

"Maybe," said Marie. "But here's another flaw: It's raining like crazy outside. We're going to get all wet and filthy crawling around in the mud looking for a crack in the foundation. Couldn't we just give Mr. Delmonico and Ms. Okeke your sketches and say that's what we think the problem is and then let professionals do their work and look for the crack?"

"You mean tell them our hypothesis without trying to prove it ourselves?" asked Charlie. "Never."

"Well, I don't like the idea of our clothes getting ruined," said Marie. "We're going to have to crawl around inside, too, in the basement of the school to look for the crack in the foundation. I'm sure the basement is dirty."

"Yes, our clothes will get dirty," shrugged Gina. "And your point is …?"

"Easy for you to say, Gina," laughed Charlie kindly. "You never have to worry about wrecking your clothes. Don't get me wrong—I love your wild outfits. They're already so broken in that they border on grunge."

"This is true," grinned Gina. "Dirt doesn't scare me."

"I'm with Gina," said Allie. "It's only *schmutz*. What's the big deal?"

"You already ruined all your clothes by accidentally dyeing them blue, Allie Oops," Marie said sharply. "I'd like to keep mine nice."

"Give me a break, Marie," snorted Allie. "You're the one who's up to your elbows in compost for your dead sticks. We're not walking through plutonium. You—"

"I know what," interrupted Izzy, eager to restore peace, as usual. "Let's wear our Bob's Auto Repair jumpsuits." When the S.MA.R.T. Squad solved the mystery of why the school was so cold, Gina had provided the girls with coveralls so they wouldn't ruin their clothes while they examined the heat ducts and vents. "Where are those, Gina? You left them up here after we wore them last time, right?"

"Uh, yeah, I think so," said Gina. "They're around here somewhere. Let me think for a second." Gina closed her eyes to concentrate. After a moment, she pulled a box out of a dark corner and flipped open the lid. "Found them," she said, "ri-i-i-i-i-ght here." She began to toss coveralls at the girls, who giggled as they caught them.

The girls put them on over their clothes. As Izzy zipped hers over her hoodie and jeggings, she was surprised to see that Marie looked pleased. "I thought you hated these getups, Marie," she said.

Marie cinched her belt tight and smiled at Izzy. "I found out that mechanics' coveralls like these are on trend right now. They're sort of like jumpsuits, which are very hot this season," she said, pulling on a knitted cap and protective gloves. Although Izzy was dead sure that was a look that would not be on trend anywhere at any time, she wisely said nothing.

But Allie teased Marie, "Ready for the runway?"

Marie smiled. She spun around, twirling on her toes, arms raised, as graceful as a ballerina—or as graceful as a ballerina in a pair of mechanics' coveralls and track shoes painted thick with phosphorescent paint could be.

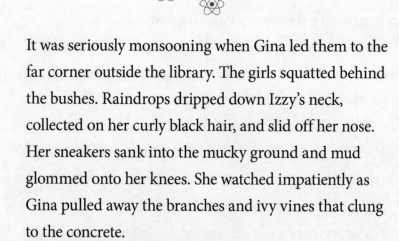

It was seriously monsooning when Gina led them to the far corner outside the library. The girls squatted behind the bushes. Raindrops dripped down Izzy's neck, collected on her curly black hair, and slid off her nose. Her sneakers sank into the mucky ground and mud glommed onto her knees. She watched impatiently as Gina pulled away the branches and ivy vines that clung to the concrete.

"Aha," Gina said at last. She ran her pointer finger up a long, thin, zig-zaggy crack. "Here is the problem."

"I'll take a picture of it," said Marie. Since it was after school, Marie was allowed to use her phone. "Now let's go.

I'm soaked to the skin."

"Me too," said Allie, agreeing with Marie for once.

"Forget these onesies. We should have worn wet suits, flippers, masks, and snorkels."

"Just a second," said Gina. She hunched protectively over the blueprints, trying to keep them dry while she marked the damaged corner with an X. Then she rolled them up, tucked them down the front of her coveralls, and stood. "Okay, now for the indoor part of our adventure."

Izzy stood up, too. She swiped her hands on the back of her legs to dry them but succeeded only in smearing mud all over the seat of her pants.

Even Charlie, who was so tall that her overalls actually fit, had mud-spattered cuffs and muddy knees. When she stood, Charlie said, "Listen. You guys wait here while I make sure the coast is clear." She laughed. "If anybody sees us coming into the school after hours and looking like this, they'll flip out—"

"And ask lots of sticky questions about what we're up to," Gina tagged on.

"Well, make it snappy, Charlie," said Marie. A strand of her hair had escaped her hat and was plastered to her cheek. "I'm drenched."

The girls huddled together behind a prickly bush until Charlie beckoned them to come inside. *Squish, squish.* The girls' wet shoes left a slick trail behind them on the tile floors as they went inside, down the stairs, and descended into the semidarkness of the basement.

"It's spooky down here," Izzy whispered, batting away a spiderweb. Even though it was soft, her voice echoed against the basement's cement walls and floor.

Gina flicked on her flashlight and held it under her chin. She looked like a specter. "Ghoulish or foolish?" she said in a deep, creepy voice. "What kind of horror show has the S.M.A.R.T. Squad fallen into this time?"

"Another disgusting one, as per usual," sniffed Marie. "It smells like old, soggy mushrooms in this basement. Don't breathe too deeply, everybody. If there's mold down here, we don't want to inhale it."

The girls held their breath as they crept forward. The basement was sort of a maze. They had to wend their way around the furnace, stacks of boxes, and piles of discarded desks and chairs. It was hard to navigate in the dim light that came through the small, dust-encrusted windows, even when Gina used her flashlight and Marie used the flashlight on her phone to beam a path of light ahead of them.

"*Ouch,*" yelped Allie. "I stubbed my toe—again. Where are we anyway?"

"We're in the Basement of No Return," moaned Izzy in her most ghostly, ghastly voice. "No one who enters ever escapes. Nooooo one."

"Ha ha," said Marie. "This place is full of dead ends. I wouldn't be at all surprised to see a dead body. I—"

Suddenly, *CRASH! THUD!* "Ohhh, HELP!" shrieked Allie. "Somebody *help!*"

7

"Eeeek!" Allie hollered, at total meltdown volume.

"What, what, what, what, what?!" yelled Charlie.

"*Shhhh!*" shushed Izzy. "Keep your voices down, or we'll get caught."

But Charlie spoke over her. "What happened? Is everyone okay?"

"*Ooof!*" Frantic, the girls bumped into each other, scrambling in the dark.

"I dropped my phone," wailed Marie.

"Ow! That's my *foot*," Izzy whispered as someone stomped on her toe.

"Stop," Gina ordered in a voice that was low but not loud. "Everybody freeze."

In the sudden silence, the only sound was a slow *drip*

... drip ... drip.

Gina swung her flashlight around like a searchlight and stopped when the light illuminated Allie, who was sprawled on the floor. Her coveralls were smeared with muck, and so were her face and her hands. "Allie, are you okay?" Gina asked, stooping to help her.

"Yeah, I guess I am," said Allie, though her voice sounded wobbly. With Gina's help she sat up. "I just—" Allie struggled to get her breath. "I just slipped in a puddle and *boom*, fell like a ton of bricks."

She tried to stand, but Charlie rushed to her side saying, "Don't move. We have to be sure you don't have a concussion. How many fingers am I holding up?"

"I don't know, Charlie," said Allie, half exasperated, half laughing. "It's so dark, I can't see my own hand in front of my face, much less yours."

"Do you think you have any broken bones?" Charlie asked. "Is anything hurt?"

"Yes," said Allie. "My pride. I'm such a klutz."

"Hey, I'm glad you're a klutz," said Gina. "Because that puddle you fell in is just what we've been looking for." Gina pointed her light into the corner above the puddle. "I figure this is the corner under the library. See the crack in the wall? And see the seepage coming in through the crack? That's it, S.M.A.R.T. Squadders. That's the source of the mold."

"Ah-*ha!*" said Izzy. "Gotcha, mold."

Marie took photos of the water dripping down the wall like a pitiful waterfall. She photographed the dark

stain of water damage creeping up the wall, too, and Gina marked the spot on her blueprints of the school.

"It's really wet down here, isn't it?" said Charlie. She lifted one foot out of the puddle on the floor and water dripped off her shoe with a desolate *plink, plink, plink*, onto the wet cement. "Our poor old Atom Middle School is dissolving into crud, washing away like a sandcastle. Probably there's no money to fix it."

Izzy added, "The damage happened because of too much rain. You can't do anything about the weather."

"Something can be done about the problem, though," said Gina.

"Like what?" asked Allie.

"Well," Gina began, "First—"

"Hey. Can we go?" Marie interrupted impatiently. "It's so dark and drippy down here, it gives me the creeps. My eyes are itchy, and I feel like that horrible mold is growing on *me*."

"Let's go to my house," said Charlie. "I'm starving, as usual, and my moms made jalapeño dip yesterday. It's so spicy that it will make your nose run worse than the mold does."

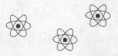

The girls rode their bikes through the rain. By the time they got to Charlie's house, they were sweaty from exertion and as wet as whales.

"Oh, my word," said Charlie's mom Susannah when she saw them at the door. "Stop right there. Don't come in yet. Give me those sopping wet coveralls, and I'll toss them in the washer. Better give me your socks, too. Leave your shoes at the door. Then grab some chips and dip and go sit in the family room."

Soon the girls were dry and comfortable, sitting in the family room around a big bowl of homemade jalapeño dip and a basket of chips. Each girl had a puppy in her lap, too. Charlie's moms were veterinarians. There were always animals at her house. The girls had met the puppies back in September when they were too young to hold. It was a treat now to cuddle a puppy apiece.

"Okay, Gina," said Allie. "Since we can't fix the crack, or the leak, or the mold ourselves, how do we tell the people who can what it is they need to do?"

"We write a report," said Gina.

"Borrrr-ing," said Marie. She held her puppy, which was asleep, next to her face and made a sleepy face herself, too. "I think it would be a lot more fun for us—and for them—if we made sort of a scrapbook with the information in it. Like, we can print out the photos that I took. Gina, you can add the blueprints that you marked and the comic strip that you drew about hydrostatic pressure. Izzy can rewrite her letter about mold making people sneeze for the scrapbook, too, as a reminder."

"I'll make a list of what can be done to stop the hydrostatic pressure problem from getting worse," added Gina.

"I'm kind of worried about all those books in the library," said Izzy, stroking her puppy's silky ears. "Do you think that because they're moldy, they'll have to be thrown away?"

"I'm sure something can be done to save them," said Charlie.

"Let's look it up," said Allie. She put her puppy down and powered up her laptop. "I bet there's lots of information about ways to clean mold off books."

While Allie researched online, Charlie's mom Laurie found the girls an empty scrapbook. Charlie printed up Marie's photos. Marie was the most artistic, so she took charge of arranging and attaching Izzy's letter, the photos, the blueprints, and Gina's comic strip, and decorating the borders of the pages. The last two pages of the scrapbook had Gina's To-Do List and the information that Allie found about removing mold from books.

To-Do List

Once mold is removed, cracks are repaired, and standing water has dried completely, here are ways to avoid hydrostatic pressure buildup again:

1. Be sure gutters and downspouts drain away from the foundation.

2. Grade the earth so that it channels water downhill, away from the foundation.

3. Use gravel as a drainage layer, so you won't have water-heavy soil pushing against foundation walls.

4. Keep caulking around doors and windows in good shape.

5. Inspect the walls and floors, and repair or seal cracks immediately.

6. Have a sump pump and drain tiles in the basement.

7. Be vigilant. Keep looking for signs of hydrostatic pressure. If you ignore it, problems will get worse, and more serious cracks and deterioration will begin.

Here's how to remove mold from books:

○ Brush off any mold from the surface of the pages.

○ Dampen a sponge or washcloth with a detergent/bleach/water mixture, and very lightly brush over the mold-contaminated areas.

○ Open the books and put them in the sun to dry. (The sun can kill many types of mold spores.)

○ Do this over and over again as often and as much as necessary.

"Stupendous," said Charlie, when the scrapbook was finished. "I'm just sayin': Good job, everybody. Props."

"It is The Best," agreed Izzy.

"Let's put it in Ms. Okeke's mail cubby in the main office and also write a note saying to share it with Mr. Delmonico," said Marie eagerly.

"I wonder what they'll do when they read this," mused Charlie.

"Well, I hope they fix the problem—and fast," said Allie. "Because, for starters, I'm sure that until the mold is gone, there'll be no science fair. And that will mean there'll be no STEM team, because we won't be able to raise money for it."

"Bummer," said Gina.

"You said it," said Allie. She added direly, "And it could be worse."

"What do you mean?" asked Marie.

"If they don't attack the problem quickly, the mold will continue to grow. Schools have had to close because of mold," said Allie.

"You mean we'd get a long vacation while they cleaned up the problem?" asked Gina. "That's not too shabby."

"No Forensics," cheered Izzy, raising her arms in triumph. "I'd be saved by the mold."

"Not so fast," said Allie. "Hold your applause. I meant some schools have to be closed permanently. The buildings are torn down."

"Oh," said Izzy. "Aw, man. I know our funky old building has its problems. I mean, first cold, now mold. But if Atom Middle School is torn down, it'll be curtains for our secret rooftop getaway."

"And death for the plants in our rooftop garden," said Charlie. She sounded as gloomy as the rainy sky outside looked.

"Wait, slow it down," said Gina. "Let's not get all emo-drama about this. They won't close the school. I mean, if they did, what would they do with all of us students?"

"They'd divide us up," said Marie. "You and I would go to Thurgood Marshall Middle School, because that's closest to where we live. Allie, Izzy, and Charlie would go to Brassy Intermediate, the brand-new one closer to where they live."

"That'd be the end of the S.M.A.R.T. Squad,"

stated Allie.

"Yes," said Izzy. "That would be the end of us."

"Our squad would be *finito*," sighed Charlie. "As if we'd never existed in the first place."

Everyone was quiet for a moment, thinking about how terrible it would be for the S.M.A.R.T. Squad to be erased.

Izzy couldn't help but think how awful it was that in solving this latest mystery one thing had led to another, as if the small flaws they'd found in the foundation of the school had become cracks so tremendous that everything was going to fall apart. What had they set in motion?

"You know how we said that S.M.A.R.T. stands for Solving Mysteries And Revealing Truths?" said Izzy. She could feel anxious, dizzy-Izzy-ness taking over. "What if we've been too smart for our own good? What if the mystery we solved and the truth we're revealing about mold does us in? What if we're the cause of our own end?"

"Like S.M.A.R.T. stands for Stupidly Mentioning A Really Terrible problem that makes So Many Awful

Rotten Things happen?" said Marie.

"Are you saying that we shouldn't tell anyone what we found?" said Charlie. "We can't do that. We're scientists. We find facts and face facts and share facts—even if we don't like them. Right?"

"Right," the rest of the girls agreed soberly.

"Okay then," said Izzy. She sounded a lot more sure than she really was. She picked up the scrapbook and hugged it to her chest. "I'll put this in Ms. Okeke's mail cubby tomorrow morning with a note about sharing it with Mr. Delmonico." She sighed. "Then we better hope the grown-ups get cooking. The sooner they solve the problem of the creeping mold, the better."

That night, Izzy couldn't sleep. It wasn't raining for a change, but storm clouds still lurked. When Izzy stared at the darkness through the skylight above her bed, she couldn't see the moon. She lay awake, thinking. Usually, her tiny, tidy room with its lofted bed, desk tucked

below, and ladder-used-as-a-bookshelf felt like a sweet, comfortable nest. But right now, it felt claustrophobic. Frustrated, worried, and restless, Izzy climbed down from her bed to get a glass of water.

Granddad was reading in the living room, sitting in his favorite chair in the soft glow of lamplight, with Izzy's fat old cat, Wickens, on his lap. Izzy wasn't surprised to find him up after midnight: Granddad taught astronomy at the local college and often sat up late to read or grade papers. Both Granddad and Wickens looked up as Izzy came into the room. "Hello, Ms. Izzy," said Granddad peering at her over the top of his reading glasses. "You remind me of the star Betelgeuse, which we astronomers think is going to explode and turn into a supernova. What's got you so wound up?"

Perched tensely on the edge of the sofa, Izzy asked, "Did you ever try to solve a problem and make a bigger problem instead?"

Granddad closed his book and gave Izzy his full attention. "Sure," he said. "It happens all the time in science. Explain."

"Well," said Izzy. "My friends and I found mold in our school. And now we're afraid that if we tell the principal, they'll close the school and tear it down."

"That's a possible outcome," nodded Granddad. "And tearing down the building would be bad because—?"

"Because, well, because it's a wacky old building," said Izzy. "I like it. And we've found a supercool secret hangout in it. Also, if the building is torn down, my friends and I and the teachers and staff and everybody will be split up and sent to different middle schools, and that'll be the end of Atom Middle School." Izzy made her fingers pop. *"Poof."*

"Ah, I see," said Granddad. "It's not just the building that you'd be sad to lose. It's what's in the building—the people, the community you're part of—that you'd miss if the school were destroyed."

"Yes, exactly," sighed Izzy, grateful to Granddad for understanding the seriousness of her problem. "And it would be all our fault, my friends and me."

Granddad took a deep breath. "A building is a big thing to try to save," he said. "And a whole community is even bigger. Maybe *too* big."

"But we have to try," said Izzy fiercely. "We can't just do nothing."

"All right," said Granddad. "You like physics, so turn to science. I'll bet you'll find a solution." He opened his book and said, "Go back to bed and think."

"Ohhh-kaaay," said Izzy. She didn't have much hope. As she climbed back into bed she thought, *A problem too big to solve. How can science help me with that?*

One of Izzy's favorite ideas in physics was string theory. It says that all objects in our universe are made up of vibrating strings and membranes of energy. Izzy loved the idea of a universe made up of quickly quivering strings. She knew how a string not only connected things but also magically created sound and music when set in motion. It seemed to her now that string theory also explained how many interconnected possibilities— like vibrating strings—spiraled up and out of the mold problem, all twisted in a gnarly knot.

Maybe that's it, she thought, her heart beating quicker. *Untangle the knot.* Maybe there was a strand— one strand—that the girls could untangle to help solve the problem. Maybe that was the way they could help.

Izzy slipped down out of bed again, turned on her desk lamp, and leafed through the scrapbook she and her friends had made. When she came to the last page, she smiled. *Yes!* She saw it now. There was something— one thing—the S.M.A.R.T. Squad could do.

8

"Whoa!" Shrieked Marie. "Don't Sit down, Charlie!"

It was early the next day. At 1 a.m. the night before, Izzy had texted the girls to meet on the roof before the first bell. The sun was shining, but the roof was pocked with puddles reflecting the puffy white clouds in the sky. There was no place dry to sit.

"This won't take long," said Izzy, getting right down to business. "Here's my idea: We're about to give the grown-ups the information they need. And while we can't repair the foundation of the school, we can repair the books that got damaged. First, I'll drop off the scrapbook, and then we'll wait and give Ms. Okeke a chance to read it. After school, we'll go to her and offer to take some of the damaged library books home and clean the mold off them."

"If we do that, won't Ms. Okeke—and everybody—know that we're the ones who discovered the mold?" asked Gina.

"No," said Izzy. "Everybody in the whole school knows about the mold now. We're just the first to volunteer to help attack the problem."

"Okay," said Charlie. "But we'll have to be careful not to make ourselves sick. Mold on books is bad."

"Charlie's right," said Allie, already reading her laptop. "Listen: 'Mold spores can be inhaled and are very harmful to the human body. When removing mold from your books, you could suffer from respiratory problems, infections, and even skin and eye irritation.'"

"Don't worry," said Marie. "I've got gloves and masks enough for all of us. And Gina, you have goggles, right?"

"I do?" asked Gina, befuddled.

"Yes, remember?" said Marie. "We used them when we solved The Mystery of the Cold School when we climbed through the ducts."

"Oh, yeah," said Gina. "I think I put those goggles back in a box with some retro hats. I know that box is in my room somewhere."

The other girls slipped one another side-glances. They knew that Gina's room was a disaster area, packed floor-to-ceiling and wall-to-wall with stuff: old computer parts, yarn and knitting needles, tools in varying states of usefulness, tap shoes, bicycle handlebars and tires, batteries, prom dresses from the 20th century, and stuffed animals, several of which Gina had equipped to be robotic.

"Not to be judgy, Gina," said Charlie gently. "But finding anything specific in the mess that's your room would require a major excavation, and probably the help of a homing device."

"You'd think," said Gina. She sounded not the least bit offended, nor the least bit conceited, either, as she said, "But remember how I found the coveralls, no sweat? I have this weird ability to think in 3D. It's as if I have a diagram of my room in my head and a photographic memory of where things are. I can almost always find what I'm looking for. I'll find the goggles."

"I hope so," said Allie. "If Ms. Okeke agrees to Izzy's suggestion and allows us to bring books home to clean, let's meet at my house Saturday. My grandmother almost always makes her fabulous, famous chocolate chip cookies on Saturdays."

"Mmmmm," sighed Charlie ecstatically.

The girls agreed to Allie's plan. And Ms. Okeke agreed to Izzy's plan, too, after she cautioned them about mold, emailed their parents to make sure they were on board, too, and made them promise to protect their eyes, noses, mouths, and hands.

On Saturday morning, the girls went to school. The janitor helped them take a few boxes of books out of the freezer in the cafeteria. Freezing didn't kill the mold, but it deactivated the spores and kept them from growing. The girls hurried to Allie's apartment building. They knew that as soon as the spores defrosted, they'd start growing again.

Thankfully, it was a sunny day. Bubbie had put her foot down and refused to allow the books inside the apartment. So the girls set up a work station in a corner of the parking lot next to Allie's apartment building. They had boxes of cold, moldy books to clean, masks and gloves provided by Marie, and goggles provided by

Gina, whose photographic memory had clearly triumphed over the chaos in her room once again. After the girls had suited up in their goggles, face masks, and gloves, Gina put her engineer's mind to work and organized them into an assembly line to repair the books.

Izzy and Marie used old toothbrushes to scrub loose mold off the pages.

Gina and Charlie used sponges slightly dampened with a mixture of detergent, bleach, and water to lightly brush over the pages that were contaminated with mold.

Allie carried the cleaned books to a sunny spot in the parking lot and opened them to dry: That way, the sun could kill off any remaining mold spores.

When the last book was done, Charlie took off her goggles and said, "Thanks for finding the goggles in that Museum of Mess that's your room, Gina. I think you *do* have a photographic memory."

"It'll come in handy," said Gina. "I'm going to be a forensic engineer, which will be totally whack."

"What's a forensic engineer?" asked Allie. The girls had taken off their gear, thoroughly scrubbed their

hands and faces, and were now seated in Allie's kitchen. Allie was passing around a plate piled high with cookies.

"Well," said Gina as she took one. "When a roof collapses or a building falls down, the forensic engineer goes in and figures out if the problem was in the design, or construction, or materials. You're sort of like a detective."

"That's the kind of forensics I like," moaned Izzy around a mouthful of cookie. "Not speeches, which I have no idea how to do."

Whenever she even thought about her Forensics class, Izzy had the sensation that she was tumbling down into a bottomless vat of dark matter. Nobody knew for sure what dark matter was, even though it made up about 30 percent of the universe. It was possibly composed of some as-yet-undiscovered subatomic particles, subject to the principle in physics called random uncertainty, which says that you can never precisely determine both the momentum and position of a particle at the same time. All that whirling darkness and random uncertainty? Add some anxiety, and that's how Izzy felt about Forensics.

But all that changed on Monday. Starting Monday, Izzy felt no uncertainty at all about Forensics. She was sure that she hated it, pure and simple. She thoroughly hated it. Because during second period on Monday, report cards were handed out. Izzy's second period class just happened to be Study Hall.

When Izzy saw the F next to Forensics, she didn't even notice that she had A's in every other course.

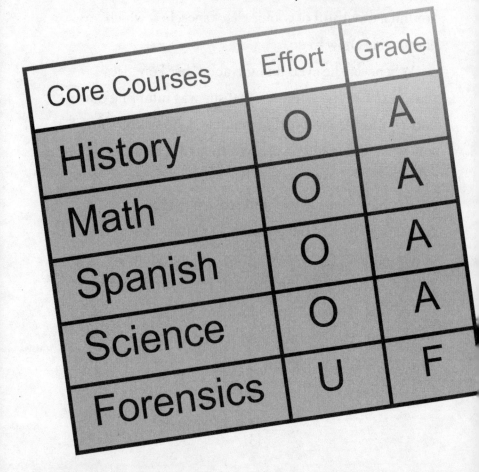

Core Courses	Effort	Grade
History	O	A
Math	O	A
Spanish	O	A
Science	O	A
Forensics	U	F

Quickly, she crumpled her report card into her fist and crumpled herself over her desk so that no one would see her humiliated face. It took all her strength not to cry. She admitted honestly to herself that she wasn't exactly surprised. But that didn't make the failure any easier to take. Because Izzy knew what the failing grade meant: She would not be on the honor roll like the rest of her friends, and she would not be able to play in the ice hockey game Saturday. That was The Worst, really— the slam to her pride about ice hockey. It was not only missing out on the game, it was also the public disgrace of being demoted to sub after being the famous inventor of The Skidizzy, the only girl on the team, the almost star. *I guess old Maddie Sharpe turned out to be right,* Izzy thought. *I will not play ice hockey.*

Ms. Martinez was merciful and didn't say anything to Izzy during Study Hall. But at the end of the period, as everyone was leaving, she said, "Izzy, please stay behind. I'd like to speak to you."

When everyone had left, Ms. Martinez began, "I understand that this failure is hard for you, Izzy. This isn't what you are used to, is it?"

Izzy shook her head miserably. "No," she said. "It's awfully embarrassing. Everybody will know I've failed when they see that I'm not playing in the hockey game."

"Ah, yes," said Ms. Martinez. "You're rather famous for being the only girl on the hockey team, aren't you? Remember when I told you that my favorite poet, Emily Dickinson, says luck is work, not chance? Well, Emily Dickinson has something to say about fame, too. She wrote: 'Fame is a bee. It has a song—It has a sting—Ah, too, it has a wing.' In other words, fame flies away."

Izzy sighed.

Ms. Martinez went on kindly, saying, "I know you like science. Well, just as science has precise requirements that must be met and standards that must be upheld, this class does, too. You knew that you were going to be graded not only on your individual presentation on a topic of your choice, but also on class participation, such as raising your hand in class, contributing when the class is divided into groups, and volunteering to make short speeches or announcements, none of which you did. If you want to pass next marking period, I've just told you how. It's up to you." She smiled. "I have absolute faith in you, Izzy. I know you can do it. Agreed?"

Izzy nodded. She was afraid that if she tried to talk, she'd cry.

"All right, you can go," said Ms. Martinez. "I'll see you in class tomorrow."

"Okay," said Izzy hoarsely.

She was surprised to see Trevor outside the door, leaning against the lockers, waiting for her.

"Hey," he said. Izzy had never seen him without a smile. He looked weird when worried. "My buddy in your Forensics class told me you might not do too well grade-wise. I just, uh, I just wanted to be sure that you're okay. Are you? Okay, I mean."

Izzy shook her head. "Nope," she said. "I'm the opposite of okay. I flunked. And before you say anything else, yes, I know that means I can't play in the game Saturday, and yes, that probably means that you'll get to sub for me. Congratulations."

Trevor looked stricken. "Izzy, that's not why I'm here," he said. "That's not what I wanted, not at all."

"I know," sighed Izzy. "Sorry to be mean. I'm just a

little bummed right now. Listen, I'll teach you The Skidizzy, like I promised. You'll need it now. You can use it in the game."

"No, I—" Trevor began.

But Izzy stopped him. "I'd *like* to teach you," she said. She managed a wobbly grin. "It'll feel good to do *some*thing well and not stink up the place like I do at Forensics."

Trevor grinned, too. "Okay then," he said. "Maybe after practice today?"

"Okay," said Izzy.

Trevor left and Izzy trudged off to lunch, though she knew there was no way she could choke down any food. She expected that her friends would be on the roof, taking advantage of their new honor roll privilege of eating wherever they wanted. But there they were—Allie, Charlie, Marie, and Gina—in the cafeteria as usual, waiting for Izzy. They greeted her with long, sad faces.

"We kind of figured you might not be on the honor roll," said Allie, "because of stupid old Forensics."

"How are you doing?" asked Charlie. She slipped Izzy a homemade granola bar to cheer her up. "We're all really, really sorry that this happened."

"Tell us about it," said Gina. "That is, if you want to."

Izzy shrugged. "There's not much to tell," she said. "I flunked, straight-out, flat-out, flunked, which means that I can't play in the ice hockey game Saturday."

"Oh, no," said Marie. "That's more toxic than the mold." She sighed. "And by the way, I think we should have slapped a big URGENT sticker on our scrapbook. It's driving me crazy that there has been no announcement about whether the school is going to close or not."

"At least they haven't canceled the science fair," said Allie.

"Not yet," said Marie. "But—"

"Listen, Izzy," Allie cut in. "We know that failing screws up hockey. But failing doesn't mean you can't participate in the science fair. While we wait to hear what's going to happen—I mean about the school closing because of mold—we can still plan our project. Can we meet at your house this afternoon?"

"Sure," said Izzy. She was surprised to find herself taking a bite of her sandwich. Somehow her friends and

Trevor had distracted her from her misery, at least a little bit. "But you'd better come a little later than usual. I have to stay after hockey practice."

"What for?" asked Gina.

"Oh," said Izzy in a breezy, offhand way. "I'm teaching The Skidizzy to that guy Trevor."

"'That guy Trevor'?" Marie repeated, eyebrows sky-high. "He's only the hottest guy in the whole school. Did you ask him or did he ask you?"

"He asked me," said Izzy.

"Izzz-*eee*," said Allie. "This is monumental! It's global! I *knew* he had a crush on you!"

"Oh, no, it's not like that," protested Izzy. "He just wants to learn how to make that shot."

"Yeah, right," said Gina, with full hipster-switch-meaning sarcasm.

"Mm-hmm, Izzy," said Charlie, nodding sagely. "I'm sure that's all—NOT."

The days were getting shorter. It was dusk when the girls gathered at Izzy's house after their sports and activities.

"Okay," said Marie to Izzy. "Spill the tea."

"We want the scoop, the whole scoop, and nothing but the scoop," added Gina.

"I thought we were meeting to talk about our science fair project," said Izzy.

"Sure, sure. We'll get to that eventually," said Charlie. "But right now, you are more important, Izzy. We want to talk about you. How'd it go with Trevor?"

"Ahhhh, Trevor," sighed Allie, batting her eyelashes and thumping her hand on her heart.

"Aw, jeesh," said Izzy. She spoke with exaggerated

patience. "I keep telling you: Trevor wants to learn The Skidizzy *because* he's going to play in the game *because* I can't *because* I flunked Forensics. End of story."

Izzy was glad that just then, her mom came in. "May I join you?" she asked.

"Yes, please," said Izzy. She snuggled next to her mom on the sofa and pulled her mom's arm around her shoulders for comfort. "We're talking about the fact that I ... I flunked Forensics."

Mom nodded, unsurprised. "Ms. Martinez sent me an email," she said. She hugged Izzy. "Sorry, honey. I know it's tough."

At Mom's kind words, Izzy eyes flooded with tears. She felt as though her emotions were bigger than she was, too big for her body to hold in. Mom handed her a tissue, and she mopped her face and blew her nose. When she could speak again, Izzy went on to explain what Ms. Martinez had said that she must do to pass next marking period. Izzy ended by saying raggedly, miserably, "I can't. I just can't. I've tried speaking out in class, and I failed, so I can't."

Mom patted Izzy's shoulder. "I can see how it may

feel that way," she said. "But your statement has a logical flaw called *post hoc, ergo propter hoc,* which means 'after this, therefore because of this.'" Izzy's mom was a lawyer. Sometimes she slipped into logic talk. "You're assuming a false cause and effect. Just because you've tried and failed, that doesn't mean you will fail again."

"And actually, Izzy, you *can* speak out," Charlie reminded her gently. "You have, twice. Remember how you stood up in front of practically the whole school in the cafeteria to suggest the STEM team? And then you spoke up again in Mr. Delmonico's office when we were changing the lightbulb to an LED bulb that wouldn't heat up the thermostat. We know that you can do it when you have to."

"You're like an ideal gas in chemistry," Marie said. "An ideal gas can expand to fill any volume, but it can only do work under pressure."

"I hate the pressure of speaking in front of a group," said Izzy. Thinking about it made her feel squirmy. "That's my fatal flaw."

"Nobody's perfect. We all have to live with our flaws," said Izzy's mom. "I myself exist hovering perpetually at the edge of hysteria about my deadlines."

"My flaw is FOMO," said Marie, with a laugh. "'Fear Of Missing Out.'"

"My flaw is FOBI," joked Gina. "'Fear Of Being Invited.'"

Then Charlie said, "You know, Iz, it seems like being hesitant to talk is not necessarily bad. If you're not talking, maybe you're listening, and that's good, right?"

"Right," said Izzy's mom and the girls.

"But it felt terrible when I flubbed my speech in Forensics class," she said. "Remember 'my spavorite fort'?" Izzy shuddered. "Everyone laughed."

"You make us laugh on purpose all the time with your dumb puns," said Allie.

"That's different," said Izzy. "I'm silly in front of you guys on purpose. You're my friends."

Izzy's mom shrugged. "I don't see how it's different," she said. "Those kids in Forensics class might be your friends, too, especially if you make them laugh. Who's to say?"

"There's a fifty-fifty chance the kids will be cool," said Allie. "No one knows what'll happen. You might as well be optimistic. I say, take the leap. Go ahead and be funny. What have you got to lose?"

"You are who you are anyway," said Charlie. "Own it."

"And if they don't get it, then that's their problem," said Marie.

"Right," said Gina. "Go out in a blaze, if not a blaze of glory, at least flaming."

Izzy laughed. "Thanks," she said sarcastically. "Now, *p-l-e-a-s-e* can we talk about something else?"

"Science fair!" said Allie.

"I'll leave you girls to it," said Izzy's mom. She gave Izzy a quick kiss, and then she left.

"Now, about our time-motion traffic project," said Allie in a no-nonsense tone. She flipped opened up her laptop. "I've assigned each of you a job, and I've made a schedule for us. If we film the buses tomorrow, which is Tuesday, and then pull an all-nighter Tuesday doing the computer analysis, then by Wednesday we'll be ready to—"

"Time-out," said Charlie. "Did you say 'pull an all-nighter Tuesday'? There's no way I can do that. We have a track meet on Wednesday after school, and if I don't get 10 hours of sleep, I'll be slow as a snail."

"Me too," said Gina.

Allie frowned. "In case you have forgotten," she said tersely, "the science fair is Wednesday night."

"Let's just make a volcano," said Marie. "It's not exactly exciting—"

"Or groundbreaking," punned Izzy. "Volcano? Groundbreaking? Get it?"

Marie rolled her eyes and continued, "But a volcano is quick and easy."

"I hear that," said Charlie. "We definitely need something quick and easy, or even better, already done. How about making a display about our rooftop garden? We could show photos of our pumpkins."

"No way!" protested Gina. "If we go public, you can kiss our private hangout goodbye. We'll never be allowed on the roof again."

"We could show how we solved the mold problem," said Charlie.

"And ruin the secret of the S.M.A.R.T. Squad?" said Izzy. "Never!"

"I'm telling you, a volcano is perfect," said Marie. "We can construct and paint the volcano and bake cookies on Tuesday and let the paint dry all day Wednesday and have the whole thing ready for Wednesday night."

"Fine with me," said ever-practical Gina. "Especially if the volcano spews out phosphorescent paint. That would be out there."

"A volcano does sound doable," said Izzy. She turned to Allie and said kindly, "Sorry about your time-motion traffic project, Allie."

"It was a good idea," said Charlie. "We just ran out of time and motion to do it."

Allie said nothing. She slammed her laptop shut, stood up, and headed for the door.

"Oh, honestly, Allie," sighed Marie. "You don't have to get all huffy."

Allie whirled around to face the girls. She looked furious. "I warned you guys over and over again that we were running out of time," she said. "But you didn't listen to me. Are you happy now, Marie? You wanted to do your dumb volcano all along. Well, now you can.

But you'll do it without me."

"Come on, Allie, don't be like that," said Charlie. "We're a team."

"Ha! Some team," said Allie. "You know, maybe it wouldn't be such a tragedy if Atom Middle School is shut down permanently and the S.M.A.R.T. Squad is kaput. Our friendship is dead already."

For a moment, everyone was so stunned that no one said anything.

Izzy got up and went to Allie. "Please don't leave," she said earnestly. "You are right. We should have listened to you. We messed up. We're sorry. But we need you, Allie." She tried to tease a smile out of Allie by saying, "You're our math whiz. Nothing adds up without you."

"That's right," said Gina. "When it comes to the S.M.A.R.T. Squad, the whole's greater than the sum of its parts."

"We need you not only for the volcano, but for the cookies," said Charlie. "You know Bubbie's recipe, and it was your awesome idea to sell the cookies in the first place. We really need that money, too. Earning money by selling cookies is our STEM team's only hope."

At the mention of STEM team, Allie's expression changed. It softened. She didn't want to give up on having a STEM team, either.

"Allie," said Gina in a winning way, "if we make a volcano, we can call Bubbie's chocolate chip cookies 'Mega Magma Lava Rocks,' and they'll sell like hot cakes."

"We'll display them on tectonic plates, get it?" joked Izzy.

"*Arrggh*," groaned Marie, clutching her throat as if Izzy's joke gagged her. "You've got to help us, Allie. The rest of us can't endure Izzy's puns without you."

At last, Allie relented. "Oh, all right," she said, still a little grumpy. "I think a volcano is totally elementary school. But okay."

"Good," said Gina. "Let's make it at my house. My room already looks like a volcano erupted in it."

The girls talked about what kind of volcano to make: The soda-and-candy kind? The kind that erupted in smoke? One made of papier-mâché, or cardboard, or dough, or clay?

But the whole time they were talking about hot lava,

gases, and eruptions, Izzy was distracted. Even after their meeting broke up and everyone went home and Izzy was in her room supposedly doing homework, she kept thinking back to the conversation about Forensics. *Were her friends right? Should she turn the whole stand-up-in-front-of-people problem on its head and deliberately try to make people laugh at her?* No. She flushed hot and sweaty with embarrassment all over again, remembering how agonizingly awful it had been when she had made a dork out of herself by saying, "My spavorite fort." Izzy promised herself: *I will never pull such a boneheaded move and leave myself open to such complete humiliation again.* If only there were a way she could make a speech while being protected by an impenetrable shield of invulnerability.

"Hey, Izz-kid." Her brothers materialized in her doorway. Lucas and Joseph were dressed in a crazy assemblage of discarded hockey gear that they kept at home: taped-together helmets and masks, mismatched gloves, and shin guards strapped on with bungee cords. Izzy almost laughed aloud. They looked like robots whose parts had exploded.

Lucas began, "Mom told us about you flun—"

Joseph cut him off. "Zip it, Lucas," he said, jabbing Lucas so hard that he gasped. Then Joseph said to Izzy, "Uh, we thought you might be bummed out about, well, you know. Come on. Grab your stick. It'll cheer you up to play driveway hockey."

"There's gear in here," said Lucas. He handed Izzy an old gym bag with yet more beat-up hockey stuff in it, and then both boys left.

Izzy hastily assembled her own crazy-in-the-extreme hockey outfit: a chest guard that was so much too big for her that it went all the way from her shoulders to her knees, a helmet covered with scratches and gouges, Day-Glo shin guards, and two left-handed gloves. As she was tying on her mask with a shoelace, she caught a glimpse of herself in her mirror and hooted. *Oh, man,* she thought. *Do I look like ridiculous or what? If the kids in my Forensics class got a load of me in this get up, they'd howl. Then I'd really need an impenetrable shield of invulnerability. Absolutely, positively.*

Izzy grinned. Suddenly, she knew exactly what to do. Absotively, posilutely.

On Tuesday, there was still no announcement about the school closing because of mold. But lots of kids at Atom Middle School were talking about something else shocking: Izzy.

Because on Tuesday morning, Izzy surprised everyone by going rogue.

It began when she poked her head into the door of the Forensics classroom and said, "Excuse me, Ms. Martinez. May I speak to the class?"

Ms. Martinez blinked, grinned, and made a sweeping gesture of welcome. "Be my guest," she said.

Every kid in the class turned to look at Izzy. She hadn't taken more than two steps into the room before gales of laughter broke out. Izzy raised both arms over her head, and the laughter increased. She just happened to have her hockey stick in her hands, and she was fully decked out in her—genuine—hockey uniform, from the helmet on her head to the bumpy socks pulled up to her knees. *Clomp, clomp, clomp.* Izzy made her way to the front of the classroom, thumping along on her hockey skates. She'd left the guards on the blades so she wouldn't scar the floor. She held up a giant hockey-gloved hand for quiet and said, "My Spavorite Fort."

"Hooray!" the kids cheered.

"Go for it, Nizzy Ewton!" shouted a kid in the back row.

Izzy grinned. She popped her mouth guard out into her hand and said, "Oops. I mean, 'My Favorite Sport.'"

The kids stamped their feet and clapped, chanting, "Izz-ee, Izz-ee," until Izzy held up both of her hands for quiet.

When the noise sank to a dull roar, Izzy said, "Why do I love ice hockey? Well, for the cool outfit, obviously. I mean, that's a no-brainer, right?" Izzy turned around slowly, and kids stamped their feet again and whistled. "You've already met my hockey stick and my mouth guard," said Izzy, waving them aloft. She pointed to each piece of gear as she named it. "Now I want you to admire my helmet, neck guard, shoulder pads, chest protector, wrist bands, elbow pads, hockey pants, shin pads, hockey socks, and last but not least …" She raised her foot and everyone shouted out, "Skates!"

"Another reason I love ice hockey is that there's lots of physics in it," Izzy went on. "And I'm a physics freak."

"Me too," a girl called out. "Physics freaks unite."

Izzy continued, "Get this: Pressure from the skate melts the ice, so that the blade's gliding on water, which refreezes as soon as the blade passes."

"Ooooh," said the kids.

"Cool, right?" said Izzy. "And whacking a hockey puck is a really good example of Newton's First Law of Motion, which is about inertia. It states that an object at rest will stay at rest and an object in motion will stay in motion until an outside force acts on it. I invented a trick shot called The Skidizzy that stays in motion until it slams against the back of the net and scores a goal."

"GOAL!" roared the kids.

"I've got two pieces of advice for you guys today," said Izzy. "First, put yourself in motion and come to the Atomics' first ice hockey game against Oaktree on Saturday. Help me cheer for the team. I won't be playing because of, well, some problems in this class. Second, come to the science fair Wednesday night, and while you're there, buy cookies to support a STEM team for Atom Middle School." Izzy flung out her arms. "If you do, you'll be almost as cool an ice-hockey-physics-freak as I am." She bowed, and the class leapt to their feet, clapping and cheering for her. "Thank you," she said, in her best Elvis imitation, "Thank you very much."

"That's what I'm talking about," said one boy.

"Go, Izzy!" said a girl. "Yours was the most totally un-boring speech we've had in here."

"EVER," added a guy in the front row.

Kids gathered around Izzy, and thumped her on her back. They swung her hockey stick, pulled on her oversize gloves and did the Macarena, and examined her saliva-slick mouth guard—from a distance, because no one wanted to touch it.

"All right, class," said Ms. Martinez. "Time to go. See you next time. And may I just say that whoever's speaking next has a tough act to follow."

After the rest of the students left, Ms. Martinez congratulated Izzy. "Good job," she said. "What made you change? What happened?"

Izzy smiled as she peeled off her gear and stowed it in her hockey bag. "I guess maybe the failing grade that you gave me was another example of Newton's First Law of Motion," she said. "It was the external force I needed to overcome inertia and move into action. It was a kick in the pants—I mean, in the hockey shorts."

Ms. Martinez laughed. "And what will you do for your next speech?" she asked. "Will you wear a suit of armor?"

"I was thinking maybe a robot suit," said Izzy, "or a space suit."

"Well, you can't hide behind a disguise every time," said Ms. Martinez. "You're going to have to be just you at some point. But this was a good first step. I knew you could do it. I'll give you an A+ for your truly outstanding effort today."

"Thanks," said Izzy.

"And I think I'll have a chat with Coach Peck," said Ms. Martinez. "I can't erase the F, but I can let him know you're not failing anymore. Maybe he can let you play in that game on Saturday."

"Oh, thank you, Ms. Martinez," said Izzy. She slung her hockey bag over her shoulder.

"Okay," said Ms. Martinez. "Off you go. You'll be late to your next class if you don't skedaddle, Ms. Skidizzy."

10

"Oh, I wish I could have seen you," said Marie. "I bet you were hysterical."

Tuesday afternoon, the girls had met at Allie's and made lots of Mega Magma Lava Rocks, also known as chocolate chip cookies. Now it was Tuesday night after dinner, and they were at Gina's, working on their volcano. They had made it out of clay shaped around a glass jar, which had worked out well. Because they were in a hurry, Gina dried the clay with a hair drier, and now they were painting it. Just for the fun of it, they were using Marie's phosphorescent paint on the outside.

"This is going to glow like crazy under the lights at the science fair tomorrow night," said Marie as she brushed wet strokes of eerie green paint onto the clay.

Charlie had some paint on her nose. "It'll look cool," she said.

"Especially when it erupts," said Izzy. She brushed a thick stroke of pink phosphorescent paint on her side of the volcano.

"I can't wait to see that," said Gina.

"Do you think the jar we put in the volcano is big enough?" asked Allie. "I think I'll pour some vinegar in it, to see if it'll hold an ounce."

"Better wait till the paint is dry," said Marie.

"Allie, I already put the baking soda, food coloring, and dish soap in the jar," said Charlie. "So don't—"

But it was too late. Allie poured an ounce of vinegar into the jar and WHOOSH! The volcano erupted in a gushy mess of red and yellow slush that exploded all over, spewing gunky chunks onto the girls.

"*Eeek!*" the girls shrieked. "Nooooo! Ewww!"

They leapt out of the way, spattering and spilling their paint all over. In her surprise, Gina knocked into the table, and *bam!* It tipped over, and the burbling volcano crashed to the floor upside down. The top was flattened and the sides smooshed. Oozy red goo spread out onto the floor like thick syrup.

"Look what you did!" Marie wailed to Allie. "The volcano is ruined."

"Sorry," Allie wailed back. "I didn't know the baking soda and stuff were already in the jar."

"I tried to tell you," said Charlie, "but you didn't listen. You just barged ahead."

All the girls looked at the disaster, paralyzed with horror. The volcano was totally blown.

"What'll we do now?" asked Izzy. "After we clean up, I mean."

"We don't have enough clay to make another volcano," said Gina. "And anyway, we don't have time."

"Oh, now we won't have anything in the science fair at all!" exclaimed Allie.

"And whose fault is that?" said Marie icily.

Izzy thought that the tension between Marie and Allie was building up to a fight that would be sort of like the biggest known black hole collision that happened about nine billion light-years away but was so huge that it was detectable on Earth.

"Hey, you guys," Izzy said. "Let's not give up. I'm sure we can think of something besides the volcano, something we can do right away."

"We could build a model of the Eiffel Tower out of toothpicks," suggested Marie, who had visited the Eiffel Tower in Paris.

"How about a solar-powered battery that powers a skateboard?" asked Charlie, always athletic.

"What about a chart that explains the Fibonacci code?" said mathematically minded Allie.

Izzy shook her head. "No, no, no," she said. "Gina's got all kinds of weird stuff here in her room. If we put our minds to it, we can make something from the stuff that's right in front of us. Come on. We've all got good brains. Let's use our heads."

"Brains? Heads?" said Gina. "I've got an idea." She smiled. "In fact, I've thought of a way we can use everybody's brain and everybody's head."

"Okay, Genius Gina," said Charlie, smiling. "Spill. Tell us your idea."

Gina was already on her hands and knees, rummaging around under her bed. She pulled out a big, beat-up box. "Remember when we were suiting up to be safe while we removed the mold from the library books?" she asked.

"Sure," said Izzy. "You gave us all swim goggles to wear to protect our eyes."

"Right," said Gina. "I got them at the secondhand store where I shop for clothes. In the box, under the goggles, I found some brand-new white bathing caps—12 dozen to be exact." She tilted the box to show the girls. "Look."

"Twelve dozen, 144, that's called a gross," Allie informed everyone briskly.

Marie wrinkled her nose. "Gross?" she asked, sounding wary. "The caps are gross?"

"No, no," laughed Gina. "That's just how many caps there are. The caps aren't gross at all. They're perfectly new and clean."

"If they're new, how come they were at the

secondhand store?" asked Charlie. "What's wrong with them?"

"They have tiny pinpricks in them," Gina explained. "That's why they were rejected, and that's how they ended up in the goggle box at the secondhand store."

"Okay, okay, *okay*," said Allie impatiently, flapping her hands. "But how do the caps solve our science fair problem?"

"It's simple," said Gina. "Everybody who stops by our table at the science fair will get a bathing cap. I'll help people put them on. Izzy, you can help, too. Then, while the person watches in a mirror, one of us will use phosphorescent paint to draw the parts of the brain on the cap. Another one of us will label the parts with a marker, and explain what each part does."

"I love it!" gushed Izzy.

"Me too!" laughed Charlie. "It's smart *and* crazy cool!"

"We've already got the bathing caps," said Izzy. "And Marie, you've got the phosphorescent paint. What else do we need to do tonight to get ready for the science fair tomorrow?"

Allie immediately powered up her laptop and clicked

on diagrams of the brain. She turned to Marie and said enthusiastically, "Marie, you should be the one to paint the caps. You're the most artistic."

"Thanks," said Marie, with a quick, pleased smile. "That'll be fun. I'll practice at home later, maybe on a shower cap."

"And Charlie, you know the most about the functions of the different parts of the brain," said Gina, "so you should label the parts and explain the functions to everyone."

"I'll read up on brain functions tonight," nodded Charlie, "to refresh my memory. And I'll bring markers to the fair tomorrow."

"Meanwhile, I'll go home and make cookies. We'll sell *millions*," crowed Allie. "We'll call the cookies 'Brain Food.'"

"Let's call our bathing-cap brains 'Thinking Caps,'" Izzy jumped in. "Get it?"

All the girls groaned at Izzy's joke until Charlie called their attention back to the matter at hand, saying, "So! It's pretty clear that we all agree. But to make it official, let's take a vote. All in favor of Gina's brainy idea, say aye!"

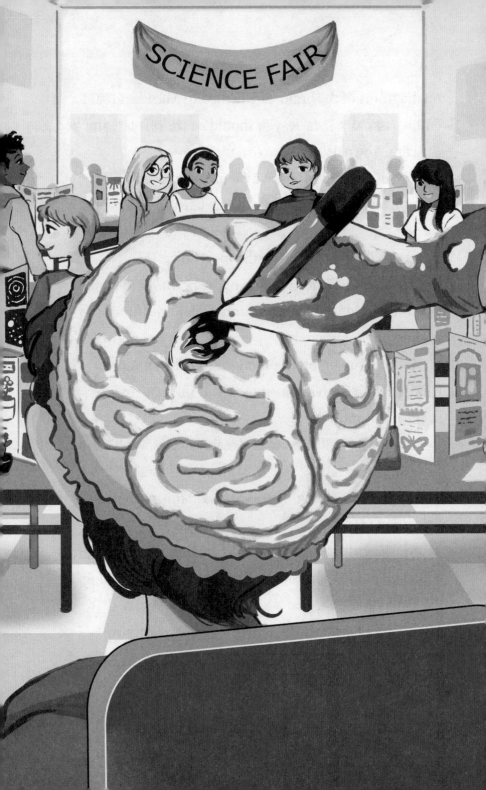

"Aye!" all five girls shouted. Allie raised both arms and danced wildly, and Marie bounced on her toes as she clapped.

"It's unanimous," said Charlie. "And I predict that after the science fair on Wednesday night, it'll also be unanimous that we've pulled off the best and funniest science fair project *ever*."

"Sure," laughed Izzy. She could not resist one final pun. "It just goes to show you how amazing we are when we put our heads together."

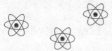

The next night the science fair was held in the cafeteria. All five girls had to work hard at their assigned tasks. It took the whole S.M.A.R.T. Squad working as a team to handle the Thinking Caps. There was always a long line of people waiting to have their brains drawn at the Thinking Caps table. Allie walked up and down the line, selling Brain Food cookies. Izzy and Gina handed out bathing caps and helped people pull them down tight and stuff their hair inside. Then the people watched in the mirror as Marie painted the parts of the brain onto their caps. Luckily, Marie had remembered to wear an old T-shirt over her clothes, because she was soon speckled with phosphorescent paint. Charlie labeled the parts of the brain with a marker as she explained what each part did.

"Everybody's loving this," Charlie said to Gina after a while. "They're getting a big kick out of their Thinking Cap brains."

"Just about all of them are buying cookies, too," said Allie, stopping by the table to refill her tray.

"This is The Best," Izzy sighed happily.

Just then, it got even better. Someone (Izzy was pretty sure it was Trevor) turned the lights off.

"Whoa!" everybody exclaimed. "Oooooh." They were delighted because the whole cafeteria was full of disembodied brains that glowed eerily in the dark.

"Oh, man!" breathed Allie. "This is *so* cool!"

Suddenly music blared through the dark. A parent was using her phone to play the Atom Middle School fight song, "The Electric Slide," and soon the disembodied brains were bouncing and swaying. In fact, the whole room was so full of dancing and singing that the walls shook. A lot of people sang the words, and others clapped to the beat.

When the music stopped, Principal Delmonico flashed the lights on and off and called out, "May I have everyone's attention, please?" It took a while for the laughter and clapping and cheering to quiet. When people had settled down, Mr. Delmonico continued, "Well, that was fun, wasn't it? Now folks, as you know, our library has been shut down because of a mold problem. We were really afraid that ALL of Atom Middle School would have to be shut down, maybe even permanently. But I am glad to tell you tonight that, thanks to quick action and excellent information, we've been able to clean up the existing mold."

"Yahoo!" everyone cheered and stamped their feet.

"Even better," Mr. Delmonico went on, "is the fact that we've already begun to address the source of the problem and fix the foundation of the school. Mold should not be a problem in the future."

Everyone cheered even louder and longer, so Mr. Delmonico had to wait and then wave his hands for quiet. At last he said, "Ms. Okeke, our librarian, has asked me to thank the sixth grade girls who volunteered to clean the mold off the contaminated books. Their quick work rescued those books. I'm sure everyone also joins me in thanking the anonymous researchers who gave us such timely and helpful information about the cause of the mold and how to prevent it from invading our school building again. Whoever it was really saved the day. In fact, they saved Atom Middle School."

Now the crowd went wild clapping and cheering. The S.M.A.R.T. Squad girls slipped pleased looks at one another. It was impossible for them not to beam happily.

Another win for the S.M.A.R.T. Squad, Izzy thought with pride and satisfaction. *Another win for science.*

When they had cleaned up after the science fair, the five friends went to the roof. It was a starry night, and the sky went on forever.

"Well," Marie pronounced. "Charlie's prediction was *partly* correct. Our S.M.A.R.T Squad did pull off the brainiest and funniest science fair project ever. But I think it's also fair to say that our Thinking Caps project made this year's science fair the best one Atom Middle School has ever—and probably *will* ever—have."

"YES!" cheered the girls, high-fiving one another.

"And the Brain Food cookies were a hit. We made fifty-seven dollars and twenty-five cents," said Allie. "Let's make another batch of cookies and sell them at the ice hockey game."

"Good idea," said Izzy. "I can help you bake but …" She grinned. "I'm afraid I won't be able to help you sell the cookies at the game. Ms. Martinez told me tonight that she talked to Coach Peck, and he said I could suit up for the game. I'll sit on the bench with the team and sub if they need me. And if I do extra credit in Forensics and get my grade up to passing, I can be in the starting lineup for the next game."

"Hooray!" cheered Marie, Charlie, Gina, and Allie. They swung their painted bathing caps on their pointer fingers so that the colors made a glowing swirl in the dark. "Way to go, Izzy!"

Gina said, "Selling the cookies won't earn us

everything we need, but it'll be a start toward supporting our STEM team."

"You mean the Atom Middle School STEM team," Charlie corrected her. "Which is sure to be a championship team."

"It will be if we're on it," grinned Marie. "The S.M.A.R.T. Squad, that is. We're good scientists."

"And good friends," added Allie.

"Yes," agreed Izzy. "The Best."

THE TRUTH BEHIND THE FICTION

NEWTON'S FLAW

THE TRUTH BEHIND THE FICTION

NEWTON'S LAWS

The title of this book, *Newton's Flaw,* is a play on Isaac Newton's Laws of Motion, which are three principles first stated by the famous scientist in 1687. Newton's laws are crucial to physics because they describe the relationship among mass, force, and motion. We can see Newton's laws at work in the physics of ice hockey.

NEWTON'S FIRST LAW: Objects at rest stay at rest and objects in motion stay in motion unless acted upon by a force. Think of a hockey puck as the object in this first law and a player with a hockey stick as the force. The hockey puck stays at rest; that is, it will not move until the player acts upon it—hits it with her stick—and transfers her energy to the puck, sending it into motion. Once in motion, the puck will not stop moving until it comes into contact with another force that acts upon it—a hockey stick, for example, or even better, the back of the goal. Score!

NEWTON'S SECOND LAW: Force equals mass multiplied by acceleration. Think of the size of a hockey player as the mass in this second law and the player's speed on the ice as the acceleration. The bigger the player and the faster her speed, the more force, or energy, she will be able to transfer to the puck through her stick. In order to have enough force, smaller players need to be fast—that is, to have extra acceleration—because they don't have as much mass.

NEWTON'S THIRD LAW: Every action has an equal and opposite reaction. Think of a skater practicing a power start. She wants it to be as fast and explosive as possible. She digs the toe of one skate into the ice behind her, crouches, and pushes back against the skate as hard as she can. The action of pushing back against the toe of her skate has the equal and opposite reaction of propelling the skater forward. The harder she pushes back, the faster she skates forward.

MOLD, A FUNGUS

QUESTION: What's not animal, vegetable, mineral, bacteria, or plant; is both microscopic and the largest living thing on Earth; and grows in a space station as well as it grows on your foot?

ANSWER: Fungus. No wonder the plural of "fungus" is "fungi," which is often pronounced FUN guy.

Mold like *Stachybotrys chartarum,* or **black mold,** is one type of fungus. (All molds are fungi, but not all fungi are molds.) More than 140,000 types of fungi have been identified so far, and there may be two million more. Your feet alone have about 100 types of fungi on them. Don't worry: All humans carry fungi in their bodies. It's totally normal.

Fungi are not animals even though, like animals, they get their energy from food. But animals must find or catch their food and then eat it. When fungi sense food nearby, they grow

Black mold

A puffball fungus releasing spores

toward it and absorb it. They break the food down by releasing digestive enzymes outside their bodies and take in only the nutrients they can use, so they don't have to get rid of waste like animals do.

Fungi are not plants, either. Fungi can't make their own energy the way plants do through photosynthesis. (Photosynthesis is the process in which plants use sunlight to turn water from the soil and carbon dioxide from the air into sugars to use as energy.)

Fungi grow on any organic material: plants, skin, fabric, or food. Every day, you breathe in millions of fungal spores (tiny particles). They're virtually impossible to see without a microscope. Spores become visible as they grow close together, spreading rapidly across a surface. And they can spread very fast. Using a high-speed camera, scientists have timed a fungal spore moving 82 feet per second (25 m/s), accelerating from zero to 56 miles an hour (90 km/h) in one-millionth of a second.

The Humongous Fungus is the largest living thing on Earth. It grows mostly underground in Oregon, U.S.A., covering about three square miles (8 sq km). That's the size of 1,500 U.S. football fields. Scientists think the Humongous Fungus is at least 2,000 years old. And it's still spreading. It grows bigger by about three feet (1 m) every year.

The Humongous Fungus is a honey agarics mushroom like this one.

MAPPING THE BRAIN

QUESTION: What's pink, wet, wrinkly, weighs three pounds (1.4 kg)—and completely controls every move you make and every thought you have, waking or sleeping?

ANSWER: Your brain.

Your brain is mission control when it comes to your life. Even when you are asleep, your brain stores memories and allows you to move, react, and feel emotions. Inside your brain, there are about 86 billion neurons. These neurons are connected by tiny pathways that send electrical and chemical messages to one another. Neurons send information to your brain and messages from your brain to your body. Though the brain is just 2 percent of your body weight, it uses about 20 percent of your energy. It has a lot to do! In fact, your brain is so powerful and complex that scientists are still unable to fully explain exactly how all of it works.

There are three main parts of the brain. Each part houses different abilities and actions:

The biggest part is the **cerebrum.** It controls voluntary muscles—those you choose to move and use—and actions like seeing, hearing, speaking, thinking, and remembering. The cerebrum is divided into two halves. The right half controls the left side of the body. The left half controls the right side of the body.

The **cerebellum** is located at the back of the brain. It controls coordination, movement, and balance. Your cerebellum helps you ride your bike, stand up, or jump without falling down.

Your **brain stem** controls the flow of messages between the brain and body and also controls basic, automatic body functions such as breathing, swallowing, digesting, heart rate, blood pressure, consciousness, and whether you're awake or snoozing. The brain stem is connected to the spinal cord, which runs down the center of your back and carries commands from your brain to your arms, legs, and trunk, like *Run, legs!* It also sends sensory information from your body back to your brain, like, *Ouch! That stove is hot!*

CEREBRUM:
Controls voluntary muscles and senses

CEREBELLUM:
Controls coordination, movement, and balance

BRAIN STEM:
Controls basic, automatic body functions and the flow of messages between the brain and the body

S.M.A.R.T. TERMINOLOGY

The S.M.A.R.T. Squad talks about all kinds of scientific and mathematical ideas. Here are some definitions:

BETELGEUSE is one of the brightest stars in the sky and at least 15 times more massive than the sun. Astronomers believe that Betelgeuse could one day become a supernova, which means that it will explode and then glow so brightly it could be visible by day and cast shadows at night.

Betelgeuse

DARK MATTER is a mystery. It makes up about 30 percent of the universe, but scientists can't see it and don't know exactly what it is. It can't be stars or planets, because it does not give off light. It's not a black hole, because black holes bend light and dark matter does not reflect or absorb light. We do know that whatever it is, dark matter has gravity. In fact, the only way we know that dark matter exists is by observing its gravitational effect on objects that we can see in space.

The cloudy center of this image is where scientists think there's dark matter.

HYDROSTATIC PRESSURE is "water pushing against walls." Water weighs about 62.5 pounds per cubic foot (1,000 kg/cu m). That's a lot of pressure—enough to crack a building's foundation, or make existing cracks bigger, or make a wall bow, buckle, or cave in. When water leaks into a building through cracks caused by hydrostatic pressure, basements flood and, sometimes, brick walls wick—or drink up—moisture into the building, which can cause mold.

Water exerts hydrostatic pressure on a dam.

RANDOM UNCERTAINTY refers to the fact that even if you painstakingly try to repeat an experiment or measurement exactly, you may get different results or readings every time. A series of measurements may differ slightly from one another because of uncontrollable changes during an experiment. The differences in measurements or results won't follow a predictable pattern—they'll be random—which means that your results will be somewhat uncertain.

WOMEN SCIENTISTS

These two National Geographic Explorers are among many scientists at work today whose studies will help our planet.

ANNE PRINGLE, MYCOLOGIST

Anne Pringle is a mycologist, fungal biologist, lichenologist, and scientist.
Pringle earned her undergraduate degree in biology and then a Ph.D. in botany and genetics. Later, she went on to study the death cap fungus.

Today, Pringle is a professor at the University of Wisconsin, where she studies the properties of fungi, their use to humans for medicine and food, and their dangers, such as toxicity. Pringle speaks all over the world about her work, which includes using tools from biology, math, and physics to film and model fungal spore movement or dispersal and exploring the birth, aging process, and death of individual fungi. She continues to study the death cap fungus, which is an invasive species, to learn about its implications for conservation.

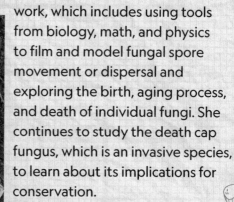

Anne and her daughter at a mushroom farm

184

FRANCESCA O'HANLON, ENGINEER

When she was in college, Francesca O'Hanlon studied civil and environmental engineering. She went on to earn her master's degree in engineering for sustainable development.

Today she is a Ph.D. researcher looking at climate change. She studies ways to help people in developing countries prepare for climate change. O'Hanlon is passionate about international development and finding ways to reduce the impact of climate change. She has worked and volunteered as a water engineer in El Salvador, Mexico, and India. While working to provide water and sanitation to displaced people in South Sudan and Central African Republic, O'Hanlon became frustrated by how difficult it was to provide clean water in places where there was no reliable supply. When she returned to school, she saw that 3D printers had become readily available, and so she began working with a team to develop low-cost technologies. In 2016,

Francesca in South Sudan, where she worked on a handwashing campaign

O'Hanlon founded Blue Tap, a social enterprise that uses 3D printing to provide household water-purifying solutions for people in developing countries.

IZZY NEWTON AND THE S.M.A.R.T. SQUAD

LAW OF CAVITIES

"Stick together," said Ms. Martinez. **"Follow me."**
She led the girls single file along the very narrow path
that zigzagged its way up the side of Sleeping Camel
Rock. The path was not terribly steep, but it was kind of
slippery from ocean spray, so the girls had to watch their
footing. The climb was worth it, though.

"Whoa," breathed Izzy when they reached the top
and walked out onto the camel's nose. The view was
spectacular. It seemed to be limitless. On three sides,
there was nothing but sea and sky and sun and sand. A
cool breeze lifted Izzy's hair off her sweaty neck and
gently sprinkled her face with spray.

After a few minutes, Izzy, Marie, Gina, and Allie walked away from the nose to explore Sleeping Camel's humps. Ms. Martinez followed them, her camera in hand and her pack slung over one shoulder.

"Look at this, Ms. Martinez," Gina said to her as she came closer. "The rock's split."

The girls were inspecting the space between the camel's humps, where there was a deep gash shaped like a V with rough, rocky sides. It was as if a huge knife had sliced the rock in two, so far down that the girls couldn't see the bottom. But they could hear water swooshing where waves swept in and out under the camel's nose. At the top, on either side of the cavity, the surface of the rocks was covered in damp moss and lichen.

"Wow, that's deep," said Ms. Martinez. As she bent over to look down into the space, her backpack slipped off her shoulder and tumbled into the abyss. "Oh, no!" she cried. She stepped forward, lost her footing on the slick moss, and slid feetfirst into the gash, waist high. "Help! My legs!" she screamed. "Girls, stay away from that edge!"

Find out more at https://kids.nationalgeographic.com/ books/smart-squad

ACKNOWLEDGMENTS:

Remember how happy Izzy felt to be part of the ice hockey team? She couldn't suppress a smile a mile wide. That's how happy I am to be part of the team developing the S.M.A.R.T. Squad books. It is an honor and a delight to work with the women at National Geographic Kids: Erica Green, Becky Baines, Shelby Lees, Sarah J. Mock, Julide Dengel, Molly Reid, and with illustrator Geneva Bowers. Everyone contributes equally and essentially; the books are a true team effort, which makes them a true joy to work on. I am so grateful!

I'm also grateful to my wonderful, articulate middle school adviser, Maggie Walsh, and my Lunch Bunch—the bright, bouncy girls at St. John the Evangelist School in Silver Spring, Maryland—who spoke with insight, empathy, and kindness about Izzy's fear of public speaking, and who provided me with creative and clever solutions to help Izzy overcome that fear. Thank you, Arsema, Kika, Nora, Madelyn, Baeza, Caroline, Emily, and Colleen, and thanks to your principal, Margaret Durney, and your teachers, Maureen Rossi and Emily Pacconi. All of you give the S.M.A.R.T. Squad books authenticity.

One of the things I love best about writing is that you never know where your best ideas and best help will come from. I spoke to a great group of students at Seneca Ridge Middle School, where my friend Ricky Peck teaches sixth grade science. It was Ricky who told me about mapping the brain on a bathing cap, an idea I love. I've dedicated this book to my friend and neighbor, Don Vannoy, who is a forensic engineer. We were chatting at a party, and when I mentioned mold, Don immediately nodded and said, "Hydrostatic pressure." I'd never heard of it. Don proceeded to provide me with excellent, useful, and detailed information, including sketches. Just the help I needed! Thank you, Don. The book is also dedicated to my niece Helen Heuer, whom I love and admire, and to whom I will always be grateful. Helen generously spoke to me for a long, long time about playing ice hockey and being on a middle school ice hockey team. It was Helen who explained the vocabulary, the equipment, the drills, how to make a slap shot, and why being small is an advantage. With humor, patience, enthusiasm, and specificity, Helen educated me. Again, she gave me just the help I needed. Thank you, Helen, with all my heart.

—Valerie Tripp